# PLANETOID 127
# AND
# THE SWEIZER PUMP

# PLANETOID 127
# AND
# THE SWEIZER PUMP

## EDGAR WALLACE

ISBN: 978-93-5336-679-7

**First Published:** 1929

LECTOR HOUSE LLP
E-MAIL: lectorpublishing@gmail.com

# PLANETOID 127
# AND
# THE SWEIZER PUMP

BY

## EDGAR WALLACE

1929

# CONTENTS

Page

**PLANETOID 127**


- CHAPTER I . . . . . . . . . . . . . . . . . . . . . . . . . . . . . . . . . . . . . . . . . .1
- CHAPTER II . . . . . . . . . . . . . . . . . . . . . . . . . . . . . . . . . . . . . . . . . .8
- CHAPTER III . . . . . . . . . . . . . . . . . . . . . . . . . . . . . . . . . . . . . . . . .14
- CHAPTER IV . . . . . . . . . . . . . . . . . . . . . . . . . . . . . . . . . . . . . . . . .19
- CHAPTER V . . . . . . . . . . . . . . . . . . . . . . . . . . . . . . . . . . . . . . . . . .24
- CHAPTER VI . . . . . . . . . . . . . . . . . . . . . . . . . . . . . . . . . . . . . . . . .29
- CHAPTER VII . . . . . . . . . . . . . . . . . . . . . . . . . . . . . . . . . . . . . . . . .33
- CHAPTER VIII . . . . . . . . . . . . . . . . . . . . . . . . . . . . . . . . . . . . . . . . .37


**THE SWEIZER PUMP**


- CHAPTER I . . . . . . . . . . . . . . . . . . . . . . . . . . . . . . . . . . . . . . . . . .44
- CHAPTER II . . . . . . . . . . . . . . . . . . . . . . . . . . . . . . . . . . . . . . . . . .60
- CHAPTER III . . . . . . . . . . . . . . . . . . . . . . . . . . . . . . . . . . . . . . . . .74

# PLANETOID 127

# CHAPTER I

"CHAP" WEST, who was never an enthusiast for work, laid down the long pole that had brought him from Bisham to the shade of a backwater west of Hurley Lock, and dropped to the cushions at the bottom of the punt, groaning his relief. He was a lank youth, somewhat short-sighted, and the huge horn-rimmed spectacles which decorated his knobbly face lent him an air of scholarship which his school record hardly endorsed.

Elsie West woke from a doze, took one glance at her surroundings and settled herself more comfortably.

"Light the stove and make some tea," she murmured.

"I'm finished for the day," grunted her brother. "The hooter sounded ten minutes ago; and cooking was never a hobby of mine."

"Light the stove and make tea," she said faintly.

Chap glared down at the dozing figure; then glared past her to where, paddle in hand, Tim Lensman was bringing the punt to the shore.

Tim was the same age as his school friend, though he looked younger. A good-looking young man, he had been head of the house which had the honour of sheltering Chapston West. They had both been school prefects at Mildram and had entered and passed out on the same day.

Tim Lensman was looking disparagingly at the tangle of bush and high grass which fringed the wooded slope.

"Trespassers will be prosecuted," he read. "That seems almost an invitation—can you see the house, Chap?"

Chap shook his head.

"No; I'll bet it is the most horrible shanty you can imagine. Old Colson is just naturally a fug. And he's a science master—one of those Johnnies who ought to know the value of fresh air and ventilation."

Elsie, roused by the bump of the punt side against the bank, sat up and stared at the unpromising landing-place.

"Why don't you go farther along?" she asked. "You can't make tea here without—"

"Woman, have you no thought before food?" demanded her brother sternly. "Don't you thrill at the thought that you are anchored to the sacred terrain of the learned Professor Colson, doctor of science, bug expert, performer on the isobar and other musical instruments and—"

"Chap, you talk too much—and I should love a cup of tea."

"We'll have tea with the professor," said Chap firmly. "Having cut through the briars to his enchanted palace, we will be served in crystal cups reclining on couches of lapis lazuli."

She frowned up at the dark and unpromising woods.

"Does he really live here?" she addressed Tim, and he nodded.

"He really lives here," he said; "at least, I think so; his driving directions were very explicit and I seem to remember that he said we might have some difficulty in finding the house—"

"He said, 'Keep on climbing until you come to the top,'" interrupted Chap.

"But how does he reach the house?" asked the puzzled girl.

"By aeroplane," said Chap, as he tied the punt to the thick root of a laurel bush. "Or maybe he comes on his magic carpet. Science masters carry a stock of 'em. Or perhaps he comes through a front gate from a prosaic road—there must be roads even in Berkshire."

Tim was laughing quietly. "It is the sort of crib old Colson would choose," he said. "You ought to meet him, Elsie. He is the queerest old bird. Why he teaches at all I don't know, because he has tons of money, and he really is something of a magician. I was on the science side at Mildram and it isn't his amazing gifts as a mathematician that are so astounding. The head told me that Colson is the greatest living astronomer. Of course the stories they tell about his being able to foretell the future—"

"He can, too!"

Chap was lighting the stove, for, in spite of his roseate anticipations, he wished to be on the safe side, and he was in need of refreshment after a strenuous afternoon's punting.

"He told the school the day the war would end—to the very minute! And he foretold the big explosion in the gas works at Helwick —he was nearly pinched by the police for knowing so much about it. I asked him last year if he knew what was going to win the Grand National and he nearly bit my head off. He'd have told Timothy Titus, because Tim's his favourite child."

He helped the girl to land and made a brief survey of the bank. It was a wilderness of a place, and though his eyes roved around seeking a path through the jungle, his search was in vain. An ancient signboard warned all and sundry that the land was private property, but at the spot at which they had brought the punt to land the bank had, at some remote period, been propped up.

"Do you want me to come with you?" asked Elsie, obviously not enamoured with the prospect of the forthcoming call.

"Would you rather stay here?" asked Chap looking up from his stove.

She gave one glance along the gloomy backwater with its weedy bed and the overhanging osiers. A water-rat was swimming across the still water and this spectacle decided her.

"No; I think I will come with you," she said; and added, "I don't like rats."

"That was a vole," said Tim, shying a stone in the direction of the swimming rodent.

Her pretty face puckered in an expression of distaste.

"It looks horribly like a rat to me," she said. Chap poured out the tea and the girl was raising it to her lips when her eyes caught sight of the man who was watching them from between the trees, and she had hard work to suppress the scream that rose to her lips.

"What is it?"

Tim had seen her face change and now, following the direction of her eyes, he too saw the stranger.

There was nothing that was in the slightest degree sinister about the stranger; he was indeed the most commonplace figure Tim had ever seen. A short, stout man with a round and reddish face, which was decorated with a heavy ginger moustache; he stood twiddling his watch chain, his small eyes watching the party.

"Hello!" said Tim as he walked toward the stranger. "We have permission to land here."

He thought the man was some sort of caretaker or bailiff of "Helmwood."

"Got permission?" he repeated. "Of course you have—which of you is Lensman?"

"That's my name," smiled Tim, and the man nodded.

"He is expecting you and West and Miss Elsie West."

Tim's eyes opened wide in astonishment. He had certainly promised the professor that he would call one day during vacation, but he had not intended taking Chap nor his sister. It was only by accident he had met his school friend at Bisham that morning, and Chap had decided to come with him.

As though divining his thoughts, the stout man went on: "He knows a lot of things. If he's not mad he's crook. Where did he get all his information from? Why, fifteen years ago he hadn't fifty pounds! This place cost him ten thousand, and the house cost another ten thousand; and he couldn't have got his instruments and things under another ten thousand!"

Tim had been too much taken aback to interrupt. "Information? I don't quite understand...?"

"About stocks and things... he's made a hundred thousand this year out of cotton. How did he know that the boll-weevil was going to play the devil with the South, eh? How did he know? And when I asked him just now to tell me about the corn market for a friend of mine, he talked to me like a dog!"

Chap had been listening open-mouthed. "Are you a friend of Mr. Colson?" he asked.

"His cousin," was the reply. "Harry Dewes by name. His own aunt's child—and his only relation."

Suddenly he made a step towards them and his voice sank to a confidential tone.

"You young gentlemen know all about him—he's got delusions, hasn't he? Now, suppose I brought a couple of doctors to see him, maybe they'd like to ask you a few questions about him... "

Tim, the son of a great barrister, and himself studying for the bar, saw the drift of the question and would have understood, even if he had not seen the avaricious gleam in the man's eyes.

"You'd put him into an asylum and control his estate, eh?" he asked with a cold smile. "I'm afraid that you cannot rely upon us for help."

The man went red.

"Not that exactly," he said awkwardly. "And listen, young fellow... " he paused. "When you see Colson, I'd take it as a favour if you didn't mention the fact that you've seen me... I'm going to walk down to the lock... you'll find your way up between those poplars... so long!"

And turning abruptly he went stumbling through the bushes and was almost at once out of sight.

"What a lad!" said Chap admiringly. "And what a scheme! And to jump it at us straight away almost without an introduction—that fellow will never need a nerve tonic."

"How did Mr. Colson know I was coming?" asked Elsie in wonder.

Tim was not prepared with an answer. After some difficulty they found the scarcely worn track that led up through the trees, and a quarter of an hour's stiff climb brought them to the crest and in view of the house.

Tim had expected to find a residence in harmony with the unkempt grounds. But the first view of "Helmwood" made him gasp. A solid and handsome stone house stood behind a broad stretch of shaven lawn. Flower beds bright with the blooms of late summer surrounded the lawn and bordered the walls of the house itself. At the farther end, but attached to the building, was a stone tower, broad and squat, and on the top of this was erected a hollow structure—criss-crossed without any apparent order or method—with a network of wires which glittered in the sunlight.

"A silver wire-box aerial!" said Chap. "That is a new idea, isn't it? Gosh, Tim! Look at the telescope!"

By the side of the tower was the bell-roof of a big observatory. The roof was closed, so that Chap's "telescope" was largely imaginary.

"Great Moses!" said Chap awe-stricken. "Why, it's as big as the Lick!"

Tim was impressed and astounded. He had guessed that the old science master was in comfortable circumstances, and knew that indeed he could afford the luxury of a car, but he had never dreamt that the professor was a man wealthy enough to own a house like this and an observatory which must have cost thousands to equip.

"Look, it's turning!" whispered Elsie.

The big, square superstructure on the tower was moving slowly, and then Tim saw two projecting cones of some crystalline material, for they glittered dazzlingly in the sunlight.

"That is certainly new," he said. "It is rather like the gadget they are using for the new beam transmission; or whatever they call it—and yet it isn't—"

As he stood there, he saw a long trench window open and a bent figure come out on to the lawn. Tim hastened towards the man of science and in a few minutes Chap was introducing his sister.

"I hope you didn't mind my coming, sir," said Chap. "Lensman told me he was calling."

"You did well to come," said Mr. Colson courteously. "And it is a pleasure to meet your sister."

Elsie was observing him closely and her first impression was one of pleasant surprise. A thin, clean-shaven old man, with a mass of white hair that fell over his collar and bushy eye-brows, beneath which twinkled eyes of deepest blue. There was a hint of good humour in his delicately-moulded face. Girl-like, she first noted his extraordinary cleanliness. His linen was spotless, his neat black suit showed no speck of dust.

"You probably met a—er—relative of mine," he said gently. "A crude fellow—a very crude fellow. The uncouth in life jars me terribly. Will you come in, Miss West?"

They passed into a wide hall and down a long, broad corridor which was lighted on one side by narrow windows through which the girl had a glimpse of a neatly flagged courtyard, also surrounded by gay flower-beds.

On the other side of the corridor, doors were set at intervals and it was on the second of these that Tim, in passing, read an inscription. It was tidily painted in small, gold lettering:

**PLANETOID 127.**

The professor saw the young man's puzzled glance and smiled. "A little conceit of mine," he said.

"Is that the number of an asteroid?" asked Tim, a dabbler in astronomy.

"No—you may search the Berlin Year Book in vain for No. 127," said the professor as he opened the door of a large and airy library and ushered them in. "There must be an asteroid—by which, young lady, is meant one of those tiny planets which abound in the zone between Mars and Jupiter, and of which, Witts

D.Q.—now named Eros—is a remarkable example. My Planetoid was discovered on a certain 12th of July—127. And it was not even an asteroid!"

He chuckled and rubbed his long white hands together.

The library with its walnut bookshelves, its deep chairs and faint fragrance of Russian leather, was a pleasant place, thought Elsie. Huge china bowls laden with roses stood in every possible point where bowls could stand. Through the open windows came a gentle breeze laden with the perfume of flowers.

"Tea will be ready in a minute," said Mr. Colson. "I ordered it when I saw you. Yes, I am interested in asteroids."

His eyes went mechanically to the cornice of the room above the stone fireplace and Tim, looking up, saw that there was a square black cavity in the oaken panelling and wondered what was its significance.

"They are more real and tangible to me than the great planetary masses. Jupiter—a vapour mass; Saturn—a molten mass, yielding the secret of its rings to the spectroscope; Vulcan—no planet at all, but a myth and a dream of imaginative and romantic astronomers—there are no intra-mercurial planets, by which I mean" —he seemed to find it necessary to explain to Elsie, for which Chap was grateful—"that between Mercury, which is the nearest planet to the sun and the sun itself, there is no planetary body, though some foolish people think there is and have christened it Vulcan—"

An elderly footman had appeared in the doorway and the professor hurried across to him. There was a brief consultation (Elsie suspected a domestic problem, and was right) and with a word of apology, he went out.

"He's a rum bird," began Chap and stopped dead. From the black cavity above the fireplace came a thin whine of sound, and then a deafening splutter like exaggerated and intensified "atmospherics."

"What is that?" whispered the girl.

Before Tim could answer, the spluttering ceased, and then a soft, sweet voice spoke:

"'Lo... Col—son! Ja'ze ga shil? I speak you, Col—son... Planetoid 127... Big fire in my zehba... city... big fire... "

There was a click and the voice ceased abruptly, and at that moment Professor Colson came in.

He saw the amazed group staring at the square hole in the wall, and his lips twitched.

"You heard—? I cut off the connection, though I'm afraid I may not get him again to-night."

"Who is he, sir?" asked Tim frowning. "Was that a transmission from any great distance?"

The professor did not answer at once. He glanced keenly and suspiciously at the girl, as though it was her intelligence he feared. And then:

"The man who spoke was a man named Colson," he said deliberately; "and he spoke from a distance of 186 million miles!"

# CHAPTER II

THEY listened, dumbfounded.

Was the old professor mad? The voice that had spoken to them was the voice of Colson...?

"A hundred and eighty-six million miles?" said Tim incredulously "But, Mr. Colson, that was not your voice I heard?"

He smiled faintly and shook his head.

"That was literally my alter ego—my other self," he said; and it seemed that he was going to say something else, but he changed the subject abruptly.

"Let us have tea," he said, smiling at Elsie. "My butler brought the alarming news that the ice cream had not arrived, but it came whilst we were discussing that tragedy!"

Elsie was fascinated by the old man and a little scared, too. She alone of that party realised that the reference he had made to the voice that came one hundred and eighty-six millions of miles was no jest on his part.

It was Chap who, in his awkward way, brought the conversation back to the subject of mysterious voices.

"They've had signals from Mars on Vancouver, sir," he said. "I saw it in this morning's papers."

Again the professor smiled.

"You think they were atmospherics?" suggested Elsie; and, to her surprise, Colson shook his head. "No; they were not atmospherics," he said quietly, "but they were not from Mars. I doubt if there is any organic life on Mars, unless it be a lowly form of vegetation."

"The canals—" began Chap.

"That may be an optical illusion," said the science master. "Our own moon, seen at a distance of forty million miles, would appear to be intersected very much as Mars seems to be. The truth is, we can never get Mars to stand still long enough to get a definite photograph!"

"From Jupiter?" suggested Chap, now thoroughly interested.

Again Mr. Colson smiled.

"A semi-molten mass on which life could not possibly exist. Nor could it come from Saturn," he went on tantalizingly, "nor from Venus."

"Then where on earth do these signals come from?" blurted Chap, and this time Mr. Colson laughed outright.

As they sat at tea, Elsie glanced out admiringly upon the brilliant-hued garden that was visible through the big window, and then she saw something which filled her with astonishment. Two men had come into view round the end of a square-cut hedge. One was the man they had seen half-an-hour previously—the commonplace little fellow who had claimed to be a relative of the professor. The second was taller and older, and, she judged, of a better class. His long, hawk-like face was bent down towards his companion, and they were evidently talking on some weighty matter, to judge by the gesticulations of the stranger.

"By Jove!" said Chap suddenly. "Isn't that Hildreth?"

Mr. Colson looked up quickly; his keen blue eyes took in the scene at once.

"Yes, that is Mr. Hildreth," he said quietly. "Do you know him?"

"Rather!" said Chap. "He has often been to our house. My father is on the Stock Exchange, and Mr. Hildreth is a big pot in the City."

Colson nodded.

"Yes, he is a very important person in the City," he said, with just a touch of hidden sarcasm in his voice. "But he is not a very important person here, and I am wondering why he has come again."

He rose quickly and went out of the room, and presently Tim, who was watching the newcomers, saw them turn their heads as with one accord and walk out of sight, evidently towards the professor. When the old man came back there was a faint flush in his cheek and a light in his eye which Tim did not remember having seen before.

"They are returning in half-an-hour," he said, unnecessarily it seemed to Elsie. She had an idea that the old man was in the habit of speaking his thoughts aloud, and here she was not far wrong. Once or twice she had the uncomfortable feeling that she was in the way, for she was a girl of quick intuitions, and though Professor Colson was a man of irreproachable manners, even the most scrupulous of hosts could not wholly hide his anxiety for the little meal to end.

"We're taking up your valuable time, Mr. Colson," she said with a dazzling smile, as she rose when tea was over and offered him her hand. "I think there's going to be a storm, so we had better get back. Are you coming with us, Tim?"

"Why, surely—" began Chap, but she interrupted him.

"Tim said he had an engagement near and was leaving us here," she said.

Tim had opened his mouth to deny having made any such statement, when a look from her silenced him. A little later, whilst Chap was blundering through his half-baked theories on the subject of Mars—Chap had theories on everything under and above the sun—she managed to speak with Tim alone.

"I'm quite sure Mr. Colson wants to speak to you," she said; "and if he does, you are not to worry about us: we can get back, it is down-stream all the way."

"But why on earth do you think that?"

"I don't know." She shook her head. "But I have that feeling. And I'm sure he did not want to see you until those two men came."

How miraculously right she was, was soon proved. As they walked into the garden towards the path leading to the riverside, Colson took the arm of his favourite pupil and, waiting until the others were ahead, he said: "Would it be possible for you to come back and spend the night here, Lensman?"

"Why, yes, sir," said Tim in astonishment. In his heart of hearts he wanted to explore the place, to see some of the wonders of that great instrument-house which, up to now, Colson had made no offer to show them. What was in the room marked "Planetoid 127"? And the queer receiver on the square tower—that had some unusual significance, he was certain. And, most of all, he wanted to discover whether the science master had been indulging in a little joke at the expense of the party when he claimed to have heard voices that had come to him from one hundred and eighty-six millions of miles away.

"Return when you can," said Colson in a low voice; "and the sooner the better. There are one or two things that I want to talk over with you —I waited an opportunity to do so last term, but it never arose. Can you get rid of your friends?" Tim nodded. "Very good, then. I will say good-bye to them."

Tim saw his companions on their way until the punt had turned out of sight round the osiers at the end of the backwater, and then he retraced his steps up the hill. He found the professor waiting for him, pacing up and down the garden, his head on his breast, his hands clasped behind him.

"Come back into the library, Lensman," he said; and then, with a note of anxiety in his voice: "You did not see those precious scoundrels?"

"Which precious scoundrels? You mean Dawes and Hildreth?"

"Those are the gentlemen," said the other. "You wouldn't imagine, from my excited appearance when I returned to you, that they had offered me no less than a million pounds?"

Tim stared in amazement at the master.

"A million pounds, sir?" he said incredulously, and for the first time began to doubt the other's reason.

"A million pounds," repeated Colson, quietly enjoying the sensation he had created. "You will be able to judge by your own ears whether I am insane, as I imagine you believe me to be, or whether this wretched relative of mine and his friend are similarly afflicted. And, by the way, you will be interested to learn that there have been three burglaries in this house during the last month."

Tim gaped. "But surely, sir, that is very serious?"

"It would have been very serious for the burglars if I had, on either occasion, the slightest suspicion that they were in the grounds," said Mr. Colson. "They would have been certainly electrified and possibly killed! But on every occasion when they arrived, it happened that I did not wish for a live electric current to surround the house: that would have been quite sufficient to have thrown out of gear the delicate instruments I was using at the time."

He led the way into his library, and sank down with a weary sigh into the depths of a large armchair.

"If I had only known what I know now," he said, "I doubt very much whether, even in the interests of science, I would have subjected myself to the ordeal through which I have been passing during the last four years."

Tim did not answer, and Mr. Colson went on: "There are moments when I doubt my own sanity—when I believe that I shall awake from a dream, and find that all these amazing discoveries of mine are the figments of imagination due, in all probability, to an indiscreet supper at a very late hour of night!"

He chuckled softly at his own little joke.

"Lensman, I have a secret so profound that I have been obliged to follow the practice of the ancient astronomers."

He pointed through the window to a square stone that stood in the centre of the garden, a stone which the boy had noticed before, though he had dismissed it at once as a piece of meaningless ornamentation.

"That stone?" he asked.

Colson nodded.

"Come, I will show it to you," he said, rising to his feet. He opened a door in what appeared to be the solid wall, and Tim followed him into the garden.

The stone stood upon an ornamental plinth and was carved with two columns of figures and letters:

**E 6 O 1 T 2 D 4 H 4 L 1 A 1 N 3 W 1 U 1 R 2 B 1 I 3 S 2**

"But what on earth does that mean?"

"It is a cryptogram," said Mr. Colson quietly. "When Heyghens made his discovery about Saturn's rings, he adopted this method to prevent himself from being forestalled in the discovery. I have done the same."

"But what does it mean?" asked the puzzled Tim.

"That you will one day learn," said the professor, as they walked back to the house.

His keen ears heard a sound and he pulled out his watch.

"Our friends are here already," he said in a lower voice.

They went back to the library and closed the door, and presently the butler appeared to announce the visitors.

The attitude of the two newcomers was in remarkable contrast. Mr. Hildreth was self-assured, a man of the world to his finger-tips, and greeted the professor as though he were his oldest friend and had come at his special invitation. Mr.

Dawes, on the contrary, looked thoroughly uncomfortable.

Tim had a look at the great financier, and he was not impressed. There was something about those hard eyes which was almost repellent.

After perfunctory greetings had passed, there was an awkward pause, and the financier looked at Tim.

"My friend, Mr. Lensman, will be present at this interview," said Colson, interpreting the meaning of that glance.

"He is rather young to dabble in high finance, isn't he?" drawled the other.

"Young or old, he's staying," said Colson, and the man shrugged his shoulders.

"I hope this discussion will be carried on in a calm atmosphere," he said. "As your young friend probably knows, I have made you an offer of a million pounds, on the understanding that you will turn over to me all the information which comes to you by—er—a——" his lip curled—"mysterious method, into which we will not probe too deeply."

"You might have saved yourself the journey," said Colson calmly. "Indeed, I could have made my answer a little more final, if it were possible; but it was my wish that you should be refused in the presence of a trustworthy witness. I do not want your millions—I wish to have nothing whatever to do with you."

"Be reasonable," murmured Dawes, who took no important part in the conversation.

Him the old man ignored, and stood waiting for the financier's reply.

"I'll put it very plainly to you, Colson," said Hildreth, sitting easily on the edge of the table. "You've cost me a lot of money. I don't know where you get your market 'tips' from, but you're most infernally right. You undercut my market a month ago, and took the greater part of a hundred thousand pounds out of my pocket. I offer to pay you the sum to put me in touch with the source of your information. You have a wireless plant here, and somewhere else in the world you have a miracle-man who seems to be able to foretell the future—with disastrous consequences to myself. I may tell you—and this you will know —that, but for the fact that your correspondent speaks in a peculiar language, I should have had your secret long ago. Now, Mr. Colson, are you going to be sensible?"

Colson smiled slowly.

"I'm afraid I shall not oblige you. I know that you have been listening in—I know also that you have been baffled. I shall continue to operate in your or any other market, and I give you full liberty to go to the person who is my informant, and who will be just as glad to tell you as he is to tell me, everything he knows."

Hildreth took up his hat with an ugly smile. "That is your last word?" Colson nodded.

"My very last." The two men walked to the door, and turned.

"It is not mine," said Hildreth, and there was no mistaking the ominous note in his tone.

They stood at the window watching the two men until they had gone out of sight, and then Tim turned to his host.

"What does he want really?" he asked.

Mr. Colson roused himself from his reverie with a start.

"What does he want? I will show you. The cause of all our burglaries, the cause of this visit. Come with me."

They turned into the passage, and as the professor stopped before the door labelled "Planetoid 127,"

Tim's heart began to beat a little faster. Colson opened the door with two keys and ushered him into the strangest room which Tim had ever seen.

A confused picture of instruments, of wires that spun across the room like the web of a spider, of strange little machines which seemed to be endowed with perpetual motion—for they worked all the time —these were his first impressions.

The room was lined with grey felt, except on one side, where there was a strip of fibrous panelling. Towards this the professor went. Pushing aside a panel, he disclosed the circular door of a safe and, reaching in his hand, took out a small red-covered book.

"This is what the burglars want!" he said exultantly. "The Code! The Code of the Stars!"

# CHAPTER III

TIM LENSMAN could only stare at the professor.

"I don't understand you, Mr. Colson," he said, puzzled. "You mean that book is a code... an ordinary commercial code?"

Colson shook his head.

"No, my boy," he said quietly; "that is something more than a code, it is a vocabulary—a vocabulary of six thousand words, the simplest and the most comprehensive language that humanity has ever known! That is why they are so infinitely more clever than we," he mused. "I have not yet learned the process by which this language was evolved, but it is certain that it is their universal tongue."

He turned with a smile to the bewildered boy.

"You speak English, probably French; you may have a smattering of German and Spanish and Italian. And when you have named these languages, you probably imagine that you have exhausted all that matter, and that the highest expression of human speech is bound up in one or the other, or perhaps all, of these tongues. Yet there is a tribe on the Upper Congo which has a vocabulary of four thousand words with which to voice its hopes, its sufferings and its joys. And in those four thousand words lies the sum of their poetry, history, and science! If we were as intelligent as we think we are, we should adopt the language of the Upper Congolese as the universal speech."

Tim's head was swimming: codes, languages, Upper Congolese and the mysterious "they."... Surely there must be something in Dawes' ominous hints, and this old man must be sick of overmuch learning. As though he realised what was passing through the boy's mind, Colson shook his head.

"No, I am not mad," he said, as he locked the book away in the safe and put the key in his pocket, "unless this is a symptom of my dementia."

He waved his hand to the wire-laden room, and presently Tim, as in a dream, heard his companion explaining the functions of the various instruments with which the room was littered. For the most part it was Greek to him, for the professor had reached that stage of mechanical knowledge where he outstripped his pupil's understanding. It was as though a professor of higher mathematics had strolled into the algebra class and lectured upon ultimate factors. Now and again he recognized some formula, or caught a mental glimpse of the other's meaning, but for the main part the old man was talking in a language he did not comprehend.

"I'm afraid you're going a little beyond me, sir," he said, with a smile, and the old man nodded.

"Yes, there is much for you to learn," he said; "and it must be learnt!"

He paused before a large glass case, which contained what looked to Tim to be a tiny model of a reciprocating engine, except that dozens of little pistons thrust out from unexpected cylinders, and all seemed to be working independent of the others, producing no central and general result.

"What is that, sir?"

Colson smoothed his chin thoughtfully.

"I'm trying to bring the description within the scope of your understanding," he said. "It would not be inexact to describe this as a 'strainer of sound.' Yet neither would it be exact."

He touched a switch and a dozen coloured lights gleamed and died amidst the whirling machinery. The hum which Tim had heard was broken into staccato dots and dashes of sound. He turned the switch again and the monotonous hum was resumed.

"Let us go back to the library," said the professor abruptly.

He came out of the room last, turned out the lights and double-locked the door, before he took his companion's arm and led him back to the library they had recently vacated.

"Do you realise, Lensman," he said as he closed the door, "that there are in this world sounds which never reach the human brain? The lower animals, more sensitive to vibratory waves, can hear noises which are never registered upon the human ear. The wireless expert listened in at the approach of Mars to the earth, hoping to secure a message of some kind. But what did he expect? A similar clatter to that which he could pick up from some passing steamer. And, suppose somebody was signalling —not from Mars, because there is no analogy to human life on that planet, but from some—some other world, big or little—is it not possible that the sound may be of such a character that not only the ear, even when assisted by the most powerful of microphones, cannot detect, but which no instrument man has devised can translate to an audible key?"

"Do you suggest, sir, that signals of that nature are coming through from outer space?" asked Tim in surprise. And Mr. Colson inclined his head.

"Undoubtedly. There are at least three worlds signalling to us," said the science master. "Sometimes the operators make some mechanical blunder, and there is an accidental emission of sound which is picked up on this earth and is credited to Mars. One of the most definite of the three comes from a system which is probably thousands of light-years away. In other words, from a planet that is part of a system beyond our ken. The most powerful telescope cannot even detect the sun around which this planet whirls! Another, and fainter, signal comes from an undetected planet beyond the orbit of Neptune."

"But life could not exist beyond the orbit of Neptune?" suggested Tim.

"Not life as we understand it," said the professor. "I admit that these signals are faint and unintelligible. But the third planet—"

"Is it your Planetoid 127?" asked Tim eagerly; and Colson nodded.

"I asked you to stay to-night," he said, "because I wanted to tell you something of vital interest to me, if not to science. I am an old man, Lensman, and it is unlikely that I shall live for many years longer. I wish somebody to share my secret—somebody who can carry on the work after I have gone into nothingness. I have given the matter a great deal of thought, passing under review the great scientists of the age. But they are mainly old men: it is necessary that I should have an assistant who has many years before him, and I have chosen you."

For a second the horrible responsibility which the professor was putting upon him struck a chill to the boy's heart. And then the curiosity of youth, the adventurous spirit which is in every boy's heart, warmed him to enthusiasm.

"That will be topping, sir," he said. "Of course, I'm an awful duffer, but I'm willing to learn anything you can teach me. It was about Planetoid 127 you wanted to speak?"

The professor nodded.

"Yes," he said, "it is about Planetoid 127. I have left nothing to chance. As I say, I am an old man and anything may happen. For the past few months I have been engaged in putting into writing the story of my extraordinary discovery: a discovery made possible by the years of unremitting thought and toil I have applied to perfecting the instruments which have placed me in contact with this strange and almost terrifying world."

It seemed as though he were going to continue, and Tim was listening with all ears, but in his definite way the old man changed the subject.

"You would like to see round the rest of the house?" he said; and the next hour was spent in strolling around the outhouses, the little farmery which formed part of the house, and the magnificent range of hothouses, for Mr. Colson was an enthusiastic gardener.

As Tim was shown from one point of interest to another, it began to dawn upon him that there was truth in Hildreth's accusation, that Mr. Colson was something of a speculator. The house and grounds must have cost thousands; the renovations which had been recently introduced, the erection of the telescope—when Colson mentioned the cost of this, the sum took his breath away—could only have been possible to a man of unlimited income. Yet it was the last thing in the world he would have imagined, for Colson was of the dreamy, unmaterial type, and it was difficult to associate him with a successful career on the Stock Exchange. When Mr. Colson opened the gates of the big garage the boy expected to see something magnificent in the way of cars; but the building was empty except for his old motor bicycle, which was so familiar to the boys of Mildram.

"No, I do not drive a car," said Colson, in answer to his question. "I have so little time, and I find that a motor-bicycle supplies all my needs."

They dined at eight. Neither during the meal nor the period which intervened before bedtime did Mr. Colson make any further reference to his discoveries. He disappeared about ten, after showing Tim to his room. The boy had undressed and was dozing off, when there came a tap at his door.

"Come in, sir," he said, and the professor entered. From his face Tim guessed that something had happened.

He set down the electric lantern he was carrying and came slowly towards the bed.

"Lensman," he said, and there was a sharp quality in his voice. "Do you remember somebody speaking... the wireless voice? I was not in the library when the call came through, so I did not hear it distinctly."

Tim recalled the mysterious voice that had spoken in the library from the aperture above the fireplace.

"Yes, sir; you told me, it was Colson—"

"I know, I know," said the professor impatiently. "But tell me how he spoke?" His tone was almost querulous with anxiety. "I only heard the end. Was it a gruff voice, rather like mine?"

Tim shook his head.

"No, sir," he said in surprise; "it was a very thin voice, a sort of whine... "

"A whine?" The professor almost shouted the question.

"Yes, sir." Colson was fingering his chin with a tremulous hand.

"That is strange," he said, speaking half to himself. "I have been trying to get him all the evening, and usually it is simple. I received his carrier wave... why should his assistant speak...? I have not heard him for three days. What did he say?"

Tim told him, as far as he could remember, the gist of the message which had come through, and for a long time the professor was silent.

"'He does not speak English very well—the assistant, I mean —and he would find a difficulty in putting into words... you see, our language is very complicated." And then, with a smile: "I interrupted your sleep."

He walked slowly to the door and stood for a while, the handle in his hand, his chin on his breast.

"If anything should happen, you will find my account in the most obvious place." He smiled faintly. "I'm afraid I am not a very good amateur mason—"

With these cryptic words he took his departure. Tim tossed from side to side and presently dropped into an uneasy doze. He dreamt that he and the professor were stalking through black, illimitable space. Around, above, below them blazed golden suns, and his ears were filled with a roar of whirling planets. Then suddenly the professor cried out in a terrible voice: "Look, look!" And there was a sharp crash of sound, and Tim sat up in bed, the perspiration streaming from every pore.

Something had wakened him. In an instant he had slipped out of bed, pulled on his dressing-gown, thrust his feet into his slippers, and had raced out into the corridor. A deep silence reigned, broken only by the sound of an opening door and the tremulous voice of the butler.

"Is anything wrong, sir?"

"What did you hear?" asked Tim quickly.

"I thought I heard a shot."

Tim waited for no more: he ran down the stairs, stumbling in the darkness, and presently came to the passage from which opened the doors of the library and the room of Planetoid 127.

The library was empty: two lights burned, accentuating the gloom. A quick glance told him that it was not here the professor was to be sought. He had no doubt that in his sleep he had heard the cry of the old man. He turned on the light in the corridor, and, trying the door of the Planetoid room, to his consternation found it was open. The room was in darkness, but again memory served him. There were four light switches near the door, and these he found. Even as he had opened the door he could detect the acrid smell of cordite, and when the light switched on he was not unprepared for the sight which met his eyes. The little machine which Colson had described as the "sound strainer" was a mass of tangled wreckage. Another instrument had been overturned; ends of cut wires dangled from roof and wall. But his eyes were for the moment concentrated upon the figure that lay beneath the open safe. It was Professor Colson, and Tim knew instinctively that the old man was dead.

# CHAPTER IV

COLSON was dead!

He had been shot at close quarters, for the hair about the wound was black and singed. Tim looked over his shoulder to the shivering butler who stood in the doorway.

"Get on the telephone to the police," he said; and, when the man had gone, he made a brief examination of the apartment.

The destruction which the unknown murderer had wrought was hurried but thorough. Half a dozen delicate pieces of apparatus, the value and use of which Tim had no idea, had been smashed; two main wires leading from the room had been cut; but the safe had obviously been opened without violence, for the key was still in the lock. It was the shot which had wakened the boy, and he realised that the safe must have been opened subsequent to the murder.

There was no need to make an elaborate search to discover the manner in which the intruder had effected his entry: one of the heavy shutters which covered the windows had been forced open, and the casement window was ajar. Without hesitation, lightly clad as he was, Tim jumped through the window on to a garden bed. Which way had the murderer gone? Not to the high road, that was certain. There could only be one avenue of escape, and that was the path which led down to the backwater.

He considered the situation rapidly: he was unarmed, and, even if the assassin was in no better shape (which he obviously was not) he would not be a match for a powerfully built man. He vaulted up to the window-sill as the shivering butler made his reappearance.

"I've telephoned the police: they're coming up at once," he said.

"Is there a gun in the house—any kind?" said Lensman quickly.

"There's one in the hall cupboard, sir," replied the man, and Tim flew along the corridor, wrenched open the door, found the shot-gun and, providentially, a box of cartridges. Stopping only to snatch an electric hand-lamp from the hall-stand, he sped into the grounds and made his way down the precipitous path which led to the river. His progress was painful, for he felt every stone and pebble through the thin soles of his slippers.

He had switched on the light of the hand-lamp the moment he had left the house, and here he was at an advantage over the man he followed, who was working in the dark and dared not show a light for fear of detection. That he was on the right track was not left long in doubt. Presently the boy saw something in his path, and, stooping, picked up a leather pocket-case, which, by its feel, he guessed contained money. Evidently in his hurry the murderer had dropped this.

Nearer and nearer to the river he came, and presently he heard ahead of him the sound of stumbling footsteps, and challenged his quarry.

"Halt!" he said. "Or I'll shoot!"

The words were hardly out of his mouth when a pencil of flame quivered ahead in the darkness, something "wanged" past his head and struck the bole of a tree with a thud. Instantly Tim extinguished his lamp. The muzzle of his gun advanced, his finger on the trigger, he moved very cautiously in pursuit.

The man must be somewhere near the river now: the ground was falling more steeply. There was no sound ahead until he heard a splash of water, the hollow sound of feet striking the bottom of a boat, and a faint "chug-chug" of engines. A motor-launch! Even as he reached the riverside he saw the dark shape slipping out towards the river under cover of the trees. Raising his gun, he fired. Instantly another shot came back at him. He fired again; he might not hit the assassin, but he would at any rate alarm the lock-keeper. Then, as the little launch reached the opening which brought it to the river, he saw it slow and come almost to a stand-still. For a second he thought the man was returning, and then the explanation flashed upon him. The backwater was choked with weeds and the little propeller of the launch must have caught them. If he could only find a boat! He flashed his lamp vainly up and down the bank.

"Plop!"

The bullet was so near this time that it stirred the hair of his head. Hastily extinguishing the light, he waited. Somebody was working frantically at the launch's propeller, and again raising his gun, he fired. This time his shot struck home, for he heard a howl of fury and pain. But in another few seconds the launch was moving again, and had disappeared into the open river. There was nothing for Tim to do now but to retrace his steps to the house. He came into the room of death, hot, dishevelled, his pyjamas torn to ribbons by the brambles through which he had struggled, to find two police officers in the room. One was kneeling by the side of the dead man; the other was surveying the damaged apparatus.

"This is the young gentleman, sir," said the shivering butler, and the officers turned their attention to Tim.

In a few words he described what he had seen, and whilst one of the policemen went to telephone a warning along to the lock-keepers, he gave an account to the other of the events of that night so far as he knew them.

"There have been several burglaries here," said the sergeant. "I shouldn't be surprised if this is the same fellow that tried to do the other jobs. Do you know anything about this?"

He held a sheet of paper to the boy, and Tim took it. It was covered with Colson's fine writing.

"It looks almost as though it were a message he'd been writing down. He'd been listening-in—the receivers are still on his ears," said the officer. "But who could tell him stuff like that?"

Tim read the message:

"Colson was killed by robbers in the third part of the first division of the day. Nobody knows who did this, but the correctors are searching. Colson said there was a great earthquake in the island beyond the yellow sea. This happened in the sixth division of the day and many were killed. This place corresponds to Japan, but we call it the Island of the Yellow Sea. The great oilfields of the Inland Sea have become very rich, and those who own the fields have made millions in the past few days. There will be—"

Here the writing ended.

"What does he mean by 'Colson was killed in the third division' or whatever it is?" said the dumbfounded policeman. "He must have known he was going to be killed... it beats me."

"It beats me, too," said Tim sadly. "Poor old friend!"

At eleven o'clock came simultaneously Inspector Bennett, from Scotland Yard, and Mr. Colson's lawyer: a stout, middle-aged man, who had some information to give.

"Poor Colson always expected such a death. He had made an enemy, a powerful enemy, and he told me only two days ago that this man would stop at nothing."

"Did he give his name?" asked the detective.

Tim waited breathlessly, expecting to hear Hildreth's name mentioned, but the lawyer shook his head.

"Why did you see him two days ago? On any particular business?"

"Yes," said Mr. Stamford, the lawyer. "I came here to make a will, by which this young gentleman was named as sole heir!"

"I?" said Tim incredulously. "Surely you're mistaken?"

"No, Mr. Lensman. I don't mind admitting that, when he told me how he wished to dispose of his property, I urged him against leaving his money to one who, I understand, is a comparative stranger. But Mr. Colson had great faith in you, and said that he had made a study of your character and was satisfied that you could carry on his work. That was the one thing which worried him, the possibility of his life's work being broken off with no successor to take it up when he put it down. There is a clause in the will which makes it possible for you to operate his property immediately."

Tim smiled sadly. "I don't know what 'operating his property' means," he said. And then, as a thought struck him: "Unless he refers to his speculations. The Stock Exchange is an unknown country to me. Has any discovery been made about the man in the motor-launch?"

Inspector Bennett nodded.

"The launch was found abandoned in a local reach of the Thames," he said. "The murderer must have landed and made his way on foot. By the way, do you know he is wounded? We found traces of blood on the launch."

Tim nodded. "I had an idea I winged him," he said. "The brute!"

Late that afternoon there was a sensational discovery: the body of a man was found, lying amidst the weeds three miles down the river. He had been shot with a revolver.

"He is our man undoubtedly," said the inspector, who brought the news. "There is a shot wound in his shoulder."

"But I did not use a rifle or a revolver," said Tim, puzzled.

"Somebody else did," said the inspector grimly. "Dead men tell no tales."

"Where was he found?"

"Near Mr. Hildreth's private landing stage—" began the inspector.

"Hildreth?" Tim stared at him open-mouthed. "Has Hildreth got a property near here?"

"Oh, yes; he has a big estate about three miles down the river." The detective was eyeing the boy keenly. "What do you know about Mr. Hildreth?"

In a few words Tim told of the interview which he had witnessed, and the detective frowned.

"It can only be a coincidence that the man was found on his estate," he said. "Mr. Hildreth is a very rich man and a Justice of the Peace."

Nevertheless, he did not speak with any great conviction, and Tim had the impression that Bennett's view of Hildreth was not such an exalted one as he made out.

Borrowing the old motor-bicycle of the science master, he rode over to Bisham and broke the news to Chap West and his sister. The girl was horrified.

"But, Tim, it doesn't seem possible!" she said. "Why should they do it? The poor old man!"

When Chap had recovered from the shock of the news, he advanced a dozen theories in rapid succession, each more wildly improbable than the last; but all his theorising was silenced when Tim told him of Colson's will.

"I'm only a kid, and absolutely unfitted for the task he has set me," Tim said quietly; "but I am determined to go on with his work, and shall secure the best technical help I can to reconstitute the apparatus which has been destroyed."

"What do you think is behind it?" asked Chap.

Tim shook his head. "Something beyond my understanding," he replied. "Mr. Colson made a discovery, but what that discovery was we have to learn. One of the last things he told me was that he had written out a full account of his investigations, and I am starting an immediate search for that manuscript. And then there is the stone in the grounds, with all those queer figures and letters which have to be deciphered."

"Have you any idea what the nature of the discovery was?" asked Chap.

Tim hesitated.

"Yes, I think I have," he said. "Mr. Colson was undoubtedly in communication with another planet!"

# CHAPTER V

"THEN it was Mars!" cried Chap triumphantly.

"Of course it was not Mars," interrupted his sister scornfully. "Mr. Colson told us distinctly that there was no life on Mars."

"Where is it, Tim?" he asked.

"I don't know." Tim shook his head. "I have been questioning his assistants—there were two at the house—but he never took them into his confidence. The only hint they can give me is that when poor Mr. Colson was listening-in to these mysterious voices he invariably had the receiving gear directed towards the sun. You know, of course, that he did not use the ordinary aerial, but an apparatus shaped like a convex mirror."

"Towards the sun?" gasped Chap. "But there can't be any life on the sun! Dash it all, I don't profess to be a scientific Johnny but I know enough of physics to see that it's as impossible for life to exist on the sun as it would be to exist in a coke oven! Why, the temperature of the sun is umpteen thousand degrees centigrade... and anyway, nobody has ever seen the sun: you only see the photoscope... "

"All this I know," said Tim, listening patiently, "but there is the fact: the receiving mirror was not only directed towards the sun, but it moved by clockwork so that it was directed to the sun at all hours of the day, even when the sky was overcast and the sun was invisible. I admit that the whole thing sounds incredible, but Colson was not mad. That voice we heard was very distinct."

"But from what planet could it be?" insisted Chap, pushing back his untidy hair and glaring at his friend. "Go over 'em all: eliminate Mars and the Sun, of course, and where is this world? Venus, Mercury, Jupiter, Saturn, Uranus, Neptune—phew! You're not suggesting that it is one of the minor planets, are you? Ceres, Pallas, Juno, Vesta...?"

Tim shook his head.

"I am as much puzzled as you, but I am going to spend my life onwards looking for that world."

He went back to the house. The body of the old man had been moved to a near-by hospital, and the place was alive with detectives. Mr. Stamford was there when he returned, and placed him in possession of a number of names and addresses which he thought might be useful to the young man.

"I don't know that I want to know any stockbrokers," said Tim, looking at the list with a wry face.

"You never know," said Mr. Stamford. "After all, Mr. Colson expected you to carry on his work, and probably it will be part of your duties to continue his operations. I happen to know that he paid minute attention to the markets."

He indicated a number of financial newspapers that lay unopened on the table, and Tim took up one, opened it and glanced down the columns. In the main the items of news were meaningless to him. All he saw were columns of intricate figures which were so much Greek; but presently his eye caught a headline:

### "BLACK SEA OIL SYNDICATE.
### CHARLES HILDRETH'S GLOOMY REPORT
### TO THE SHAREHOLDERS.

"A meeting of the Black Sea Oil Syndicate was held at the Cannon Street Hotel yesterday afternoon, and Mr. Hildreth, Chairman of the Company, presiding, said that he had very little news for the shareholders that was pleasant. A number of the wells had run dry, but borings were being made on a new part of the concession, though there was scarcely any hope that they would be successful."

Tim frowned. Black Sea Oil Syndicate...? Hildreth? He put a question to the lawyer.

"Oh, yes," said Mr. Stanford. "Hildreth is deep in the oil market. There's some talk of his rigging Black Seas."

"What do you mean by 'rigging'?" asked Tim.

"In this case the suggestion, which was made to me by a knowledgeable authority," said Mr. Stamford, "is that Hildreth was depressing the shares issuing unpromising reports which would induce shareholders to put their shares on the market at a low figure. Of course, there may be nothing in it: Black Sea Oils are not a very prosperous concern. On the other hand, he may have secret information from his engineers."

"Such as—?" suggested Tim.

"They may have struck oil in large quantities on another part of the property and may be keeping this fact dark, in which case they could buy up shares cheaply, and when the news was made known the scrip would go sky-high and they would make a fortune."

Tim read the report again. "Do you think there is any chance of oil being found on this property?"

Stamford smiled. "I am a lawyer, not a magician," he said good-humouredly.

After he had gone, Tim found himself reading the paper: the paragraph fascinated him. Black Sea Oil...

Suddenly he leapt to his feet with a cry. That was the message which Mr. Colson had written on the paper—the Oilfields of the Inland Sea!

He ran out of the room and went in search of Stamford.

"I am going to buy Black Sea Oils," he said breathlessly. "Will you tell me what I must do?"

In a few moments the telephone wire was busy.

Mr. Hildreth had not been to his office that day, and when he strolled in to dinner, and the footman handed him his paper, he opened the page mechanically at the Stock Exchange column and ran his eyes down the list of quotations. That morning Black Sea Oils had stood in the market at 3s. 3d., and almost the first note that reached his eye was in the stop-press column.

"Boom in Black Sea Oils. There have been heavy buyings in Black Sea Oil shares, which stood this morning in the neighbourhood of 3s., but which closed firm at 42s. 6d."

Hildreth's face went livid. His great coup had failed!

In the weeks which followed the death and funeral of Professor Colson, Tim found every waking minute occupied. He had enlisted the services of the cleverest of scientists, and from the shattered apparatus one of the most brilliant of mechanical minds of the country was rebuilding the broken instruments. Sir Charles Layman, one of the foremost scientific minds in England, had been called into consultation by the lawyer, and to him Tim had related as much as he knew of Professor Colson's secret.

"I knew Colson," said Sir Charles; "he was undoubtedly a genius. But this story you tell me takes us into the realm of fantasy. It isn't possible that life can exist on the sun; and really, young gentleman, I can't help feeling that you have been deceived over these mysterious voices."

"Then three people were deceived," said Tim firmly. "My friend Chap West and his sister both heard the speaker. And Mr. Colson was not the kind of man who would descend to trickery."

Sir Charles pursed his lips and shook his head.

"It does seem most extraordinary. And frankly, I cannot understand the functions of these instruments. It is quite possible, as Colson said, that there are sounds come to this earth so fine, and pitched in such a key, that the human ear cannot catch them. And I am pretty sure that what he called a 'sound strainer' was an amplifier on normal lines. But the mysterious world—where is it? Life in some form may exist on a planetoid, but it is almost certain that these small masses which whirl through space in the zone between Mars and Jupiter are barren globules of rock as dead as the moon and innocent of atmosphere. There are a thousand-and-one reasons why life could not exist on these planetoids; and of course the suggestion that there can be life on the sun is preposterous."

He walked up and down the library, smoothing his bushy white beard, his brows corrugated in a grimace of baffled wonder.

"Most scientists," he said at last, "work to the observations of some pet observer—did the Professor ever mention an astronomer whose calculations he was endeavouring to verify?"

Tim thought for a moment.

"Yes, sir, I remember he spoke once or twice of Professor Watson, an American. I remember once he was lecturing to our school on Kepler's Law, and he mentioned the discoveries of Mr. Watson."

"Watson?" said Sir Charles slowly. "Surely he was the fellow who thought he found Vulcan, a planet supposed by some people to revolve about the sun within the orbit of Mercury. As a matter of fact, what he saw, during an eclipse of the sun, was the two stars, Theta and Zeta Cankri, or, more likely, the star 20 Cankri, which must have been somewhere in the position that Watson described on the day he made his discovery."

Then he asked, with sudden interest:

"Did Professor Colson believe in the existence of Vulcan?"

Tim shook his head. "No, sir, he derided the idea."

"He was right," nodded Sir Charles. "Vulcan is a myth. There may be intra-Mercurial bodies revolving about the sun, but it is extremely unlikely. You have found no data, no photographs?"

The word "photograph" reminded Tim. "Yes, there is a book full of big enlargements, but mostly of a solar eclipse," he said. "They were taken on Friday Island last year."

"Would you get them for me?" asked Sir Charles, interested.

Tim went out and returned with a portfolio, which he opened on the table. Sir Charles turned picture after picture without speaking a word, then he laid half a dozen apparently similar photographs side by side and pored over them with the aid of a magnifying-glass. They were the conventional type of astronomical photo: the black disc of the moon, the bubbling white edges of the corona; but evidently Sir Charles had seen something else, for presently he indicated a speck with a stylo.

"These photographs were taken by different cameras," he said. "And yet they all have this."

He pointed to the pin-point of white which had escaped Tim's observation. It was so much part of the flame of the corona that it seemed as though it were a spark thrown out by one of those gigantic irruptions of ignited gas that flame up from the sun's surface.

"Surely that is a speck of dust on the negative?" said Tim.

"But it is on all the negatives," said Sir Charles emphatically. "No, I cannot be sure for the moment, but if that is not Zeta or Theta Cankris—it is too large for the star 20 Cankris—then we may be on the way to rediscovering Professor Colson's world!"

At his request, Tim left him, whilst, with the aid of charts and almanacs, he plunged into intricate calculations.

When Tim closed the door and came into the corridor he saw the old butler waiting.

"Mr. Hildreth is here, sir," said the man in a low voice, as though he also suspected the sinister character of the financier. "I've put him in the blue drawing-room: will you see him, sir?"

Tim nodded and followed the servant.

Hildreth was standing by a window, looking out upon the lawn, his hands behind him, and he turned, with a quick, bird-like motion as he heard the sound of the turning handle.

"Mr. Lensman," he said, "I want a few words with you alone."

The young man dismissed the butler with a gesture.

"Well, sir?" he asked quietly.

"I understand that you have engaged in a little speculation. You are rather young to dabble in high finance," drawled Hildreth.

"Do you mean Black Sea Oils?" asked Tim bluntly.

"I had that stock in mind. What made you buy, Mr. Lensman—or rather, what made your trustee buy, for I suppose that, as you're under age, you would hardly carry out the transaction yourself."

"I bought because I am satisfied that Black Sea Oils will rise."

A slow smile dawned on Hildreth's hawklike face.

"If you had come to me," he said coolly, "I could have saved you a great deal of money. Black Sea Oils to-day stand at fifty shillings: they are worth less than fivepence! You are little more than a boy," he went on suavely, "and I can well understand how the temptation to gamble may have overcome you. But I was a friend of Colson's, and I do not like the thought of your money being wasted. I will take all the stock off your hands, paying you at the price you paid for it."

"That is very generous of you," said Tim drily, "but I am not selling. And as for Mr. Colson being a friend of yours—"

"A very good friend," interrupted the other quickly, "and if you tell people that he and I were enemies it may cost you more than you bargain for!"

There was no mistaking the threat in his tone, but Tim was not to be brow-beaten.

"Mr. Hildreth," he said quietly, "nobody knows better than you that you were bad friends with Mr. Colson. He was constantly spoiling your market—you said as much. You believed that he was possessed of information which enabled him to operate to your detriment, and you knew this information came by wireless, because you had listened-in, without, however, understanding the language in which the messages came. You guessed there was a code, and I believe that you made one or two efforts to secure that code. Your last effort ended in the death of my friend!"

# CHAPTER VI

HILDRETH'S face went white.

"Do you suggest that I am responsible for Colson's death?"

"You were responsible directly and indirectly," said Tim. "You sent a man here to steal the code-book—a man who has been identified this afternoon as a notorious criminal. Whether you told him to shoot, or whether he shot to save his skin, we shall never know. The burglar was killed so that he should not blab."

"By whom?" asked Hildreth steadily.

"You know best," was the curt reply.

Tim opened the door and stood waiting. The man had regained some of his composure, and, with an easy laugh, walked into the corridor. "You will hear from me again," he said.

"Thank you for the warning," was Tim's rejoinder.

After he had seen his unwelcome visitor off the premises, Tim went in search of Stamford, who, with his two assistants, was working in a little study getting out particulars of the old man's investments. The lawyer listened in silence while Tim narrated what had passed.

"He is a very dangerous man," said Mr. Stamford at last; "and, so far from being rich, I happen to know that he is on the verge of ruin. There are some queer stories about Hildreth. I have had a hint that he was once in an Australian prison, but, of course, there is no evidence to connect him with this terrible crime. What are your immediate plans?"

"The voice amplifier has been reconstituted," said Tim. "The experts are making a test to-day, though I very much doubt whether they will succeed in establishing communication."

A smile fluttered at the corner of the lawyer's mouth.

"Do you still believe that Mr. Colson was in communication with another planet?"

"I'm certain," said Tim emphatically.

He went back to the blue drawing-room, and had hardly entered before Sir Charles came in.

"It is as I thought," said the scientist; "neither Zeta nor Theta! It is, in fact, a distinct body of some kind, and, in my judgment, well outside the orbit of the hypothetical Vulcan. If you look at the back of the photograph—"

He turned it over, and Tim saw that, written in pencil in the microscopic calligraphy of the Professor, were a dozen lines of writing.

"I knew, of course, that this was a dead world, without atmosphere or even water. There can be no life there. I made an enlargement by my new process, and this revealed a series of flat, rocky valleys."

"What the deuce his new process was, heaven only knows!" said Sir Charles in despair. "Poor Colson must have been the most versatile genius the world has known. At any rate, that disposes of the suggestion that this planetary body is that whence come the signals—if they come at all."

Sir Charles waited until the experts had finished the work of reassembling two of the more complicated machines; but, though experimenting until midnight, they could not establish communication, and at last, with a sense of despair, Tim ordered the work to cease for the night.

The whole thing was becoming a nightmare to him: he could not sleep at nights. Chap and his sister came over in the morning to assist him in a search, which had gone on ever since the death of Professor Colson.

"We can do no more," said Tim helplessly, "until we have seen the Professor's manuscript. Until then we do not know for what we are searching."

"What about that stone in the garden? Won't that tell you anything?" asked Chap. "I'd like to see it."

They went out into the courtyard together and stood before the stone in silence.

**E 6 O 1 T 2 D 4 H 4 L 1 A 1 N 3 W 1 U 1 R 2 B 1 I 3 S 2**

"Of course, that isn't as difficult as it appears," said Chap, to whom cryptograms were a passion. "There is a sentence written there, containing so many 'e's', so many 'h's', etcetera, and perhaps, when we find the sentence, the mystery will be half solved."

He jotted the inscription down in a notebook, and throughout the day was puzzling over a solution. Night came, and the two were on the point of departure, when Chap said suddenly: "Do you think you were wise, Timothy, to tell the reporter Johnny all you did?"

(Tim had given an interview to a local newspaper, which had described more fully than he had intended—more fully, indeed, than his evidence at the inquest—what had happened immediately preceding Colson's death.)

"Because, y' know, it struck me," said Chap, "that the poor old Professor's manuscript would be very valuable to a certain person. Does it occur to you that our friend might also be searching for this narrative?"

This was a new idea to Tim.

"Why, yes," he said slowly; "I never thought of that. No; that didn't strike me. But I don't know where he would find it. We've taken out every likely stone in the building; I've had the cellars searched—"

"What makes you think it's behind a stone?" asked Chap.

"His reference to a mason. My guess—and I may not be far wide of the mark—is that Mr. Colson, having written his manuscript, hid it in one of the walls. But so far I have not been able to discover the hiding-place."

He walked to the end of the drive to see his friends off, and then returned to the study. He was alone in the house now, save for the servants. Sir Charles had gone back to town by the last train, and Stamford had accompanied him.

The butler came in to ask if he wanted anything before he went to bed, and Tim shook his head.

He had taken up his quarters in a spare room immediately above the library, and for an hour after his visitors had departed he sat on the broad window-seat, looking down into the courtyard, now bathed in the faint radiance of the crescent moon. The light shone whitely upon the cryptogram stone, and absent-mindedly he fixed his eyes upon this, the least of the old man's mysteries. And then—was his eye playing tricks with him? He could have sworn he saw a dark figure melt out of the darkness and move along the shadow of the box hedge.

He pushed open the casement window, but could see nothing.

"I'm getting jumpy," he said to himself, and rising with a yawn, took off his coat preparatory to undressing. As he did so, he glanced out of the window again and started. Now he was sure: he could see the shapeless black shadow, and it was moving towards the cryptogram stone.

His pulse beat a little quicker as he watched. There was no doubt about it now. In the moonlight the figure in the long black coat and the broad sombrero which shaded his face, stood clearly revealed. It was touching the stone, and even as Tim looked the little obelisk fell with a crash.

In a second Tim was out of the room and speeding along the corridor. As he came into view of the figure, it stooped and picked something from the ground.

The manuscript! What a fool he had been! That was where the old man had concealed the story of his discovery! But there was no time for regret: the mysterious visitant had already disappeared into the shadows. Was he making for the river? Tim was uncertain. He was halfway down the slope before he realised that he had made a mistake. Behind him he heard the soft purr of a motor-car, and, racing up the slope, he came into view of a red tail-light as it disappeared down the broad drive towards the road. The great iron gates were closed, and that would give him a momentary advantage, though he knew he could not reach the car before they were open.

Then he remembered Colson's motor-bicycle: he had left it leaning against the wall and had forgotten to bring it in after the trip he had made to Bisham that morning. Yes, there it was! He had hardly started the machine going when he heard a crash. The unknown had driven his car through the frail iron gates and was flying along the road to Maidenhead.

Tim came out in pursuit and put his machine all out. The car ahead gained until it came to the foot of a long and tiring hill, and then the gap between them closed. Once the driver looked back, and a minute later something dropped in the road. Tim only just avoided the spare tyre, which had been thrown overboard to trip him.

The car reached the crest of the hill as Tim came up to its rear, and, heedless of danger, stretched out his hand, and, catching hold of the hood, let the motor-bicycle slip from between his knees.

For a second he held on desperately, his feet swinging in the air, and then, with an effort, he threw his leg over the edge of the hood and dropped breathlessly on to the seat behind the driver. At first the man at the wheel did not realise what had happened, and then, with a yell of rage, he turned and struck blindly at the unauthorised passenger.

The blow missed him by a fraction of an inch, and in another second his arm was around the driver's neck. The car swayed and slowed, and then an involuntary movement of the man revealed the whereabouts of the manuscript. Tim thrust into the inside-pocket and his fingers touched a heavy roll of paper. In a flash the packet was in his hand, and then he saw the moonlight gleam on something which the man held.

The car was now almost at a standstill, and, leaping over the side, Tim plunged into the hedge by the side of the road. As he did so, he heard the "zip!" of a bullet and the patter of leaves. He ran on wildly, his breath coming in short gasps. To his ears came the blundering feet of his pursuer. He was out of breath and in no condition to meet the murderous onrush of his enemy.

And then, as he felt he could not go a step farther, the ground opened underneath his feet and he went down, down, down. For a second he lost consciousness. All that remained of his breath was knocked from his body, and he could only lie and gape at the starlit sky.

# CHAPTER VII

LOOKING up, he saw a head and shoulders come over the edge of the quarry into which he had fallen. Apparently the man was not prepared to take the risk of following, for presently the sound of his footsteps died away and there was silence.

He lay for half-an-hour motionless, recovering his breath. Although his arm was bruised he could move it and no bones were broken. At the end of his rest he rose cautiously to his knees and explored the position so far as it was revealed by the moonlight.

He had fallen twenty or thirty feet down a steep, chalky slope; but he was by no means at the bottom of the quarry face, and he had to move with the greatest care and circumspection. Presently, however, he found a rough path, which seemed to run interminably upwards. It was nearly half-an-hour later when he came to the road. The car was gone, and he walked back the way he had come, hoping that he would be able to retrieve his motor-bicycle intact, though he had his doubts whether it would be usable. To his delight, when he came upon the machine, he discovered it had suffered little damage other than twisted handlebars. His run home was without event.

Apparently his hasty exit had been heard, for the house was aroused and two manservants were searching the grounds when he came in.

"I heard the gate go smash, sir," said the butler, explaining his wakefulness. "Lord! I'm glad to see you back. Somebody's thrown over that stone in the courtyard... "

He babbled on, and Tim was so glad to hear the sound of a human voice that he did not interrupt him.

There was no sleep for him that night. With successive cups of strong coffee, brought at intervals, he sat poring over the manuscript, page by page, almost incredulous of his own eyes and senses. The sunlight poured in through the windows of the little study and found him still sitting, his chin on his palms, the manuscript before him. He had read it again and again until he knew almost every word. Then, locking the papers away in the safe, he walked slowly to the instrument room, and gazed in awe at this evidence of the dead man's genius.

Something within him told him that never in future would human speech pulsate through this network of wires; never again would that queer little amplifier bring within human hearing the thin sounds of space. Even the code was gone: that vocabulary, reduced with such labour to a dictionary of six thousand words.

He turned the switch and set the little machine working; saw the multicoloured lights gleam and glow. This much the mechanics had succeeded in doing. But the words that filtered through light and charcoal would, he thought, be dead for everlasting. He turned another switch and set something working which Sir Charles had described as a miniature air pump, and stood watching absent-mindedly as the piston thrust in and out. If he only had one tenth of Colson's genius!

His hand had gone out to turn the switch that stopped the machine, when:

"Oh, Colson, why do you not speak to me?"

The voice came from the very centre of the machine. There was no visible microphone. It was as though the lights and the whirling wheels had become endowed with a voice. Tim's heart nearly stopped beating.

"Oh, Colson," wailed the voice, "they are breaking the machines. I have come to tell you this before they arrive. He is dead—he, the master, the wizard, the wonderful man... "

The servant! Mr. Colson had told him that it was the servant who had spoken. The astral Colson was dead. How should he reply?

"Where are you?" he asked hoarsely, but there was no answer, and soon he understood why. Presently:

"I will wait for you to speak. When I hear you I will answer. Speak to me, Colson! In a thousand seconds... ."

A thousand seconds! Colson had told him once that wireless waves travel at the same speed as light. Then he was a hundred and eighty million miles away, and a thousand seconds must pass—nearly seventeen minutes—before his voice could reach through space to the man who was listening.

How had he made the machine work? Perhaps the mechanism had succeeded before, but there had been nobody at the other end—wherever the other end might be. And then:

"Oh, Colson, they are here... goodbye!"

There came to him the sound of a queer tap-tap-tap and then a crackle as though of splintered glass, and then a scream, so shrill, so full of pain and horror, that involuntarily he stepped back. Then came a crash, and silence. He waited, hardly daring to breathe, but no sound came. At the end of an hour he turned off the switch and went slowly up to his room.

He awoke to find a youth sitting on the edge of his bed. He was so weary and dulled that he did not recognize Chap, even after he spoke.

"Wake up: I've got some news for you, dear old bird," said Chap, staring owlishly through his thick, heavy glasses. "There's a Nemesis in this business—you may have heard of the lady—Miss Nemesis of Nowhere. First the burglar man is killed and then his boss is smashed to smithereens."

Tim struggled up. "Who?" he asked. "Not Hildreth?"

Chap nodded.

"He was found just outside Maidenhead, his car broken to bits —they think his steering-wheel went wrong when he was doing sixty an hour. At any rate, he smashed into a tree, and all that's left of his machine is hot iron!"

"Hildreth! Was he killed?" Chap nodded.

"Completely," he said callously. "And perhaps it's as well for him, for Bennett was waiting at his house to arrest him. They've got proof that he employed that wretched burglar. Do you know what time it is? It's two o'clock, you lazy devil, and Sir Charles and Stamford are waiting to see you. Sir Charles has a theory—"

Tim swung out of bed and walked to the window, blinking into the sunlit garden.

"All the theories in the world are going to evaporate before the facts," he said. Putting his hand under his pillow, he took out the Professor's manuscript. "I'll read something to you this afternoon. Is Elsie here?"

Chap nodded. "I'll be down in half-an-hour," he said.

His breakfast was also his luncheon, but it was not until after the meal was over, and they had adjourned to the library, that he told them what had happened in the night. Bennett, who arrived soon after, was able to fill in some of the gaps of the story.

"Hildreth," he said, "in spite of his wealth and security, was a crook of crooks. It is perfectly true that he was tried in Australia and sent to penal servitude. He had got a big wireless plant in his house, and there is no doubt that for many years he has made large sums of money by picking up commercial messages that have been sent by radio and decoding and using them to his own purpose. In this way he must have learnt something about Mr. Colson's correspondent—he was under the impression that Colson received messages in code and was anxious to get the code-book. By the way, we found the charred remnants of that book in the car. It was burnt out, as you probably know. That alone would have been sufficient to convict Hildreth of complicity in the murder. Fortunately, we have been saved the trouble of a trial."

"None of the code remains?" asked Tim anxiously. The detective shook his head.

"No, sir, none. There are one or two words—for instance, 'Zeiith' means 'the Parliamentary system of the third decade,' whatever that may mean. It seems a queer sort of code to me."

"That is very unfortunate," said Tim. "I had hoped to devote my time to telling the history of this strange people, and the book would have been invaluable."

"Which people is this?" asked Sir Charles puzzled. "Did our friend get into communication with one of the lost tribes?"

Tim laughed, in spite of himself. "No, sir. I think the best explanation I can offer you is to read Mr. Colson's manuscript, which I discovered last night. It is one of the most remarkable stories that has ever been told, and I'll be glad to have you here, Sir Charles, so that you may supply explanations which do not occur to me."

"Is it about the planet?" asked Sir Charles quickly, and Tim nodded.

"Then you have discovered it! It is a planetoid—"

Tim shook his head. "No, sir," he said quietly. "It is a world as big as ours."

The scientist looked at him open-mouthed.

"A world as big as ours, and never been discovered by our astronomers? How far away?"

"At its nearest, a hundred and eighty million miles," said Tim.

"Impossible!" cried Sir Charles scornfully. "It would have been detected years ago. It is absolutely impossible!"

"It has never been detected because it is invisible," said Tim.

"Invisible? How can a planet be invisible? Neptune is much farther distant from the sun—"

"Nevertheless, it is invisible," said Tim. "And now," he said, as he took the manuscript from his pocket, "if you will give me your attention, I will tell you the story of Neo. Incidentally, the cryptogram on the stone reads: 'Behind the sun is another world!'"

# CHAPTER VIII

TIM turned the flyleaf of the manuscript and began reading in an even tone.

## "THE STORY OF NEO."

"My name" (the manuscript began) "is Charles Royton Colson. I am a Master of Arts of the University of Cambridge, science lecturer to Mildram School, and I have for many years been engaged in the study of the Hertzian waves, and that branch of science commonly known as radiology. I claim in all modesty to have applied the principles which Marconi brought nearer to perfection, when wireless telegraphy was unknown. And I was amongst the pioneers of wireless telephony. As is also generally known, I am a mathematician and have written several text-books upon astronomy. I am also the author of a well-known monograph on the subject of the Inclinations of the Planetary Orbits; and my treatise on the star Oyonis is familiar to most astronomers.

"For many years I engaged myself in studying the alterations of ellipses following the calculations and reasonings of Lagrange, who to my mind was considerably less of a genius than Professor Adams, to whom the credit for the discovery of Neptune should be given... "

Here followed a long and learned examination of the incidence of Neptune's orbit, as influenced by Uranus.

"...My astronomical and radiological studies were practically carried on at the same time. In June, 1914, my attention was called to a statement made by the Superintendent of the great wireless telegraph station outside Berlin, that he had on three separate occasions taken what he described as 'slurred receptions' from an unknown station. He gave excellent technical reasons why these receptions could not have come from any known station, and he expressed the opinion, which was generally scoffed at, that the messages he had taken came from some extra-terrestrial source. There immediately followed a suggestion that these mysterious dashes and dots had come from Mars. The matter was lost sight of owing to the outbreak of the European War, and when, in 1915, the same German engineer stated that he had received a distinct message of a similar character, the world, and particularly the Allied world, rejected the story, for the credibility of the Germans at that period did not stand very high.

"A year later, the wireless station at Cape Cod also reported signals, as did a private station in Connecticut; whilst the Government station at Rio de Janeiro reported that it had heard a sound like 'a flattened voice.' It was obvious that these stories were not inventions, and I set to work on an experimental station which I had been allowed to set up at the school, and after about six months of hard toil I succeeded in fashioning an instrument which enabled me to test my theories. My main theory was that, if the sound came from another world, it would in all probability be pitched in a key that would be inaudible to human ears. For example, there is a dog-whistle which makes no sound that we detect, but which is audible to every dog. My rough amplifier had not been operating for a week when I began to pick up scraps of signals and scraps of words —unintelligible to me, but obviously human speech. Not only was I able to hear, but I was able to make myself heard; and the first startling discovery I made was that it took my voice a thousand and seven seconds to reach the person who was speaking to me.

"I was satisfied now that I was talking to the inhabitants of another world, though, for my reputation's sake, I dared not make my discovery known. After hard experimental work, I succeeded in clarifying the voices, and evidently the person at the other end was as anxious as I to make himself understood and to understand the nature of his unknown correspondent's speech.

"You may imagine what a heart-breaking business it was, with no common vocabulary, invisible to one another, and living possibly in conditions widely different, to make our meaning clear to one another. We made a start with the cardinal numbers, and after a week's interchange we had mastered these. I was then struck with the idea of pouring a glass of water from a tumbler near to my microphone, and using the word 'water.' In half-an-hour I heard the sound of falling water from the other end and the equivalent word, which will be found in the vocabulary. I then clapped my hands together, and used the word 'hand.' With these little illustrations, which took a great deal of time, began the formation of the dictionary. In the Neo language there are practically no verbs and few adjectives. Very much is indicated by a certain inflexion of voice; even the tenses are similarly expressed; and yet, in spite of this, the Neothians to whom I spoke had no very great difficulty, once I had learnt the art of the inflexion, in supplying the English equivalent.

"All the time I was searching the heavens in the vain endeavour to discover the exact location of this world, which was, from the description I had, exactly the same size as ours, and therefore should have been visible. I had maps of the southern hemispheres, reports from the astronomers of Capetown and Brisbane, but they could offer me no assistance. It was certain that there was in the heavens no visible planetary body as big as Neo.

"The chief difficulty I had lay in the fact that the voices invariably came from the direction of the sun; and it was as certain as anything could be that life could not exist on that great golden mass. Notwithstanding this, unless my mirror was turned to the sun, I received no message whatever; and even in the middle of the night, when I was communicating with Neo, it was necessary that I should follow, the sun's course.

"Then came the great eclipse, and, as you know, I went to the South Sea Islands to make observations. It was our good fortune to have fine weather, and at the moment of total eclipse I took several particularly excellent photographs, some of which you will find in the portfolio marked 'L.' In these and photographs taken by other astronomers, you will see, if you make a careful observation, close to the corona, a tiny speck of light, which at first I thought was my world, but which afterwards I discovered was a dead mass of material upon which it was impossible for life to exist.

"One night, when I was turning over the matter in my mind, and examining each photograph in the study of my house on the Thames, the solution flashed on me. This tiny speck, which was not a star, and was certainly not Vulcan, was the satellite of another world, and that world was moving on the same orbit as our own earth, following exactly the same course, but being, as it was, immediately opposite to us behind the sun, was never visible! On whatever part of the ellipse we might be, the sun hid our sister world from us, and that was why the voice apparently came from the sun, for it was through the solar centre that the waves must pass. Two earths chasing one another along the same path, never overtaking, never being overtaken, balancing one another perfectly! It was a stupendous thought!

"I conveyed to my unknown friend, who called himself Colson, though I am under the impression that that was due to a misconception on his part as to what Colson meant—he probably thought that 'Colson' was the English word for 'scientist'—and I asked him to make observations. These he sent to me after a few days, confirming my theory. It was after we had begun to talk a little more freely, and my acquaintance with the language had increased so that I could express myself clearly, that it occurred to me there was an extraordinary similarity both in our lives and our environment. And this is the part in my narrative which you will find difficult to believe—I discovered that these two worlds were not only geographically exact, but that the incidents of life ran along on parallel lines. There were great wars in Neo, great disasters, which were invariably duplicated on our earth, generally from two to three days before or after they had happened in this new world. Nor was it only the convulsions of nature that were so faithfully reproduced. Men and women were doing in that world exactly as we were doing in ours. There were Stock Exchanges and street cars, railways, aeroplanes, as though twin worlds had produced twin identities; twin inspirations.

"I learnt this first when my friend told me that he had been seeking me for some time. He said that he had had a broken knee some five years ago, and during his enforced leisure he had pointed out the possibility of his having another identity. He said he was frequently feeling that the person he met for the first time was one in reality whom he had seen before; and he was conscious that the thing he did to-day, he had done a week before. That is a sensation which I also have had, and which every human being has experienced.

"But to go back to the story of his having been laid up with a broken knee. He had no sooner told me this than I realised that I also had had a broken knee—I had a spill on my motor-bicycle—and that I had spent the hours of my leisure pondering the possibility of there being another inhabited planet! There is a vulgar expression, frequently met with amongst neurotic people, that they have twin souls. In very truth this man was my twin soul: was me, had lived my life, thought my thoughts, performed every action which I performed. The discovery staggered me, and I began to fear for my reason; so I went to London and consulted an eminent Harley Street specialist. He assured me that I was perfectly normal and sane, and offered me the conventional advice that I should go away for a holiday.

"Then one day my astral friend, Colson, incidentally mentioned that there was great excitement in his town because a man had bought some steel stock which had since risen considerably in price—he mentioned the name—and, glancing through a newspaper, I saw the name of a stock which sounded very similar to that of which he had told me. Moreover, the price was very much as he had mentioned it; and the wild idea occurred to me that if happenings were actually duplicated, I might possibly benefit by my knowledge. With great trepidation I invested the whole of my savings, which were not very considerable, in these shares, and a few days later had the gratification of selling out at a colossal profit. I explained to my friend at the next opportunity what I had done, and he was considerably amused, and afterwards took an almost childish delight in advising me as to the violent fluctuations in various stocks. For years I have bought and sold with considerable benefit to myself. Not only that, but I have been able to warn Governments of impending disasters. I informed the Turkish Government of the great Armenian earthquake, and warned the Lamborn Shipping Company of the terrible disaster which overtook one of their largest liners—though I was not thanked for my pains.

"After this had been going on for some years, I was prepared to learn that my friend had incurred the enmity of a rich man, whom he called Frez on his side, and that this had been brought about unwittingly through me. For this is a curious fact: not everything on this new world is three days in advance of ours. Often it happened that the earth was in advance, and I was able, in our exchanges, to tell him things that were happening here which had not yet occurred in Neo, with the result that he followed my example, and in the space of a year had become a very rich man.

"Colson, as I called him, had a servant, whose name I have never learnt; he was called the equivalent to 'helper,' and I guess, rather than know, that he is a much younger man than my double, for he said that he had been to school as a pupil of Colson's. He too learnt quickly; and if there is any difference in the two worlds, it is a keener intelligence: they are more receptive, quicker to grasp essentials.

"There are necessarily certain differences in their methods of government, but these differences are not vital. In Neo men are taught the use of arms, and receive their guerdon of citizenship (which I presume is the vote) only on production of a certificate of proficiency. But in the main their lives run parallel with ours. The very character of their streets, their systems of transportation, even their prison system, are replicas of those on this earth. The main difference, of course, is that their one language is universal. I intend at a later date writing at greater length on the institutions of Neo, but for the moment it is necessary that I should set down particulars of the machines and apparatus employed by me in communicating with our neighbours..."

Here followed twenty closely-written pages of technical description. Tim folded the manuscript and looked around at the astonished faces. Stamford was the first to break the silence.

"Preposterous!" he spluttered. "Impossible! Absurd!... It's a nightmare! Another world—good God!"

"I believe every word of it." It was Sir Charles's quiet voice that stilled the agitated lawyer. "Of course, that is the speck by the side of the corona! Not the world which poor Colson found, but the moon of that world."

"But couldn't it be visible at some time?"

Sir Charles shook his head. "Not if it followed the exact orbit of the earth and was placed directly opposite—that is to say, immediately on the other side of the sun. It might overlap at periods, but in the glare of the sun it would be impossible to see so tiny an object. No, there is every possibility that Colson's story is stark truth."

He took the manuscript from Tim's hand and read rapidly through the technical description.

"With this," he said, touching the paper, "we shall be able to get into communication with these people. If we only had the vocabulary!" he groaned.

"I am afraid you will never hear from Neo again, sir," said Tim quietly, and told of that brief but poignant minute of conversation he had had before the cry of the dying servant, and the crash of broken instruments, had brought the voice to an abrupt end.

After the lawyer and the scientist had departed, he went with Elsie into the instrument room, and they gazed in silence upon the motionless apparatus.

"The link is broken," he said at last; "it can never be forged again, unless a new Colson arrives on both earths."

She slipped her arm in his.

"Aren't you glad?" she asked softly. "Do you want to know what will happen to-morrow or the next day?"

He shivered. "No. I don't think so. But I should like to know what will happen in a few years' time, when I'm a little older and you're a little older."

"Perhaps we'll find a new world of our own," said Elsie.

# THE SWEIZER PUMP

# CHAPTER I

THE directors' office of the firm of Grennett, Carlew & Company, Ltd., was a handsome apartment, though curiously enough it was Grennett's taste which was responsible for the white and gold panelling of the wall, the harmony of the big grey-blue carpet, and the almost classical dignity of the decorations.

There were people who gave the credit to Carlew, for all that there was of luxury in the apartment, for they argued that a "grump"—as Grennett was, without doubt—could not be possessed of an artistic sense.

Herein they ignored the indisputable lessons of history, for your artist is usually a most disagreeable person.

So to Grennett the credit must for the colour scheme, and for the choice of position. The office was on the top floor of a building which commanded a view of Green Park. It was—unlike most top floors—lofty and spacious, and if the big arm-chairs were just a little too luxurious, and one desk, at least, ornate and just a trifle effeminate, you must blame Carlew, that excellent man. Yet you may absolve him at least of the flower which ornamented his desk, for it owed its presence to a force within the office, which, if he created, he could not control.

On a bright spring morning, "our Mr. Gold" was warming his hands before the fire which blazed cheerfully at one of the two fireplaces which occupied a place at either end of the room, and between whiles, when he was not engaged in giving directions to his youthful subordinate as to the disposal of the morning mail, his eyes moved from the flower-decked writing-table of the junior partner to the shabby ink-stained desk which was ever an unpleasant reminder of a very unpalatable fact—namely, that Mr. Grennett moved and had his being.

Gold was a man of twenty-five, tall and well-dressed. His face was smooth, and save for a wisp of fair moustache the contour of his jaw betrayed a certain weakness.

It was not difficult to assign his position in this firm of engineers, for he was the managing clerk to the life. He glanced contemptuously at the empty grate at the other end of the room.

"Only one fire," he said, with a twist of his head; "I wonder old Granite doesn't freeze to death. It would take a lot to freeze him," he added with a yawn.

The sycophantic youth grinned sympathetically.

"Tired, Mr. Gold?"

Gold nodded.

"Yes, had a late night," he said with a touch of patronage.

"That baby of yours?'"

Gold eyed him severely.

"Don't take a liberty, Skillett," he replied. "Because I treat you as an equal I don't want you to come it on me."

Skillett wriggled in embarrassment.

"I beg your pardon; no liberty intended, I'm sure."

Mr. Gold arranged his neck-tie in the mirror above the fireplace,

"No," he said, after a while. "If you want to know, I had a bit of a barney in the West End—late dinner and music hall, and finished up at one of them—one of those Soho clubs."

He was a purist whenever he could remember to be.

The youth gazed at him admiringly.

"That's life if you like," he said, with a note of regret in his voice. "I played dominoes all the evening and won tuppence."

Mr. Gold smiled benevolently.

"Your turn'll come," he said, then with a sudden start, "who's that?"

Skillett went to the door and looked out whilst Gold assumed a sudden industry.

"Only Miss Callington," reported the subordinate.

Gold relaxed with a little sigh of relief.

"Oh—Grennett is getting on my nerves. Phew—I shall want the tail of the dog that bit me this morning—look at my 'and!"

He extended it shakily.

He could have wished that Mr. Grennett would go away for another six months' business trip. The office had been a little heaven with only Sir, Carlew in charge.

"A gentleman, if ever there was one," he said, half to himself, as he sorted the papers on Grennett's desk.

"Mr. Carlew?"

"Who do you think I mean? No trouble, no fuss—everything goes smooth and nice—it's more like a happy family than anything else."

The door of the office opened and he raised his eyes apprehensively. The newcomer was a girl, slim and pretty. Her face was pale and in her eyes was the shadow of sorrow. She was neatly dressed and had the indefinable stamp of gentle breeding.

Gold nodded.

"Good morning, Miss Callington. Working late last night?"

"Yes; I had some letters to type for Mr. Carlew," she said quietly, but did not meet his frank stare of admiration.

"Ah! I thought you must have been. The caretaker tells me you left the light burning over your typewriter."

She looked up from the desk at which she was laying out the correspondence of the junior partner with a startled, frightened frown.

"Did I? That was careless."

"And Mr. Carlew left the light over his," said the complacent Gold; "so I put two and two together—you know my methods, Watson?"

The girl laughed nervously.

"Here, this letter had better go before Granite—I'd granite him, if I had my way—shove it over there, Miss C.—in that basket on the table." He indicated a small table by the wall. "It's that man who says he invented the Sweizer Pump."

He looked at his watch.

"Ten o'clock! Skillett, go and see if all the clerks are in."

When the door closed behind him he walked round to the girl.

"How do you like that watch, Miss C?"

She looked at it listlessly.

"It's very nice," she admitted.

"A present from Mr. Carlew," said the other, with an effort to appear careless. "Read that: 'To my friend, George Gold—in token of my regard for his loyal services.' His friend!" Gold's voice shook with genuine emotion. "Why, a man would die for Mr. Carlew."

For the first time she regarded him with interest.

"He is very good—very good indeed," she said thoughtfully; "a great-hearted man—I wish—"

She hesitated.

"Ah, so do I—now if the other chap—"

So far he got when a sharp voice in the outer office froze up the wells of eloquence and set him working feverishly. The door opened, and there came into the directors' room the subject of his thoughts: a man, tall, grim, and calmly efficient. This you read in the thin, black moustache, in the square jaw and the poise of his head. There was no smile, no hint of softening in the composition of the senior partner. His voice when he spoke was firm and not unmusical, and his keen, grey eyes had an attraction peculiarly their own.

He walked straight to his desk, peeling his gloves.

"Where's the mail?"

Grennett was laconic to the point of brutality, and the flurried Mr. Gold darted to the little table by the wall.

"I'm sorry, sir; here it is."

Grennett tapped the desk before him. "Here," he said, "is the place for it."

"I'm very sorry."

"Don't be sorry — be intelligent."

Gold took a long breath and offered the information that Mr. Carlew hadn't come yet.

The other looked up.

"He would be here, wouldn't he?"

"Yes, sir."

"Sitting at the desk?"

"Quite so, sir."

Grennett nodded carelessly.

"Don't make conversation, Gold. I don't want to talk about anything but business in office hours."

"Swine!" said Mr. Gold — but he said it to himself.

Grennett pushed a letter across the table.

"Put that aside for me — that makes the second time he has written."

"Which is that, sir?"

"The letter from the man who says we stole his patent. It may be blackmail — probably is — give it me back, I suppose we didn't steal his patent?"

He asked the monstrous question calmly, and Mr. Gold's smile was one of intense amusement.

"It's the sort of thing," he said reminiscently, "that you're bound to get in a successful business. I remember some years ago —"

"Send this to Debenham's." The senior partner had no inclination for reminiscences. — "Answer — this — and this — and this. The usual reply — we have gone into the matter and cannot take up the patents — send back the specifications."

"Yes, sir; it's a waste of time reading 'em."

Mr. Gold, it may be observed, was persistent in his desire to earn his master's approval.

"I read them last night," said Grennett quietly. "Nothing is a waste of time, except talking."

Gold moved to the door.

"Er — Gold!"

"Yes, sir."

"Do you drink!"

"Drink?" repeated the injured Gold.

"What do you think I said?"

"Well, I drink like other men—very little—I know when I've had enough."

"You've had enough when you've had none," Grennett eyed him coldly. "You've had too much when you've had any—in business hours—that will do."

He dismissed the man with a nod, but Gold felt an explanation was due. "Well, sir, I—"

"That will do—you're not a fool, you understand what I mean—oh, Gold, send Miss Callington—take these letters with you. By the way, Gold, referring to the Sweizer Pump—have you ever seen Mr. Sweizer?"

"No, sir; yes, sir."

The subordinate was taken off his guard.

"Which is it?"

"Yes, sir, I saw him once."

"What sort of man was he?"

"Oh—er," said Gold vaguely, "tall man, rather stout."

"Beard?"

"Yes, sir—yes, sir, sort of beard, I wonder he doesn't turn up again, sir; but you know what foreigners are."

Saying which, Mr. Gold felt he had justified any eccentricity of the absent Sweizer.

Left to himself, the senior partner took a cigarette from a box on the table, and lit it.

He was in the middle of a letter, writing quickly, when the girl came into the room.

"Sit down a moment, please, I want to finish this note."

She sat down, her notebook on her knees, looking into space. So Grennett found her when he had finished his letter, and for a few moments he had time to study the unconscious girl, till, aware of his scrutiny, she turned in confusion.

"Oh, I'm sorry."

He looked at her sharply.

"What is the matter with you?"

His voice, never pleasant to her, sounded harsh.

"Nothing—I'm very sorry."

"Are you ill?" he persisted.

She shook her head.

"No, Mr. Grennett—I—I am a little tired."

"You've been working late, I hear—why was this?"

She was betrayed into a gesture of impatience.

"Oh, it was last night," she said quickly. "I'm sorry Mr. Carlew left his light—"

"Working late last night—where?—not here?"

"Yes—no, well, yes. I was working here. Mr. Carlew had some letters."

"What letters?" asked the other.

"Private letters," she replied desperately, and rose to her feet. "Really, Mr. Grennett, you ask such questions—it concerned Mr. Carlew."

He nodded.

"It concerns me, too—I am a partner in this business. I know a little about business, you know—have you any family trouble?"

He saw by the colour in her cheek that she was growing angry.

"Really, Mr. Grennett," she flamed, "with due respect to you, I cannot see how my affairs can possibly interest you."

"I don't suppose you can," he said drily. "Late hours at my office are my affairs: you are using my paper, my typewriter, my stamps—half mine at any rate."

She shook her head, impatience and weariness in the movement.

"We didn't use any paper."

He looked at her keenly.

"Oh—*we* didn't!"

"I mean—I mean—" she corrected herself hastily, "I used private paper— Mr. Carlew's private paper." She rose half-hysterically. "I will not be bullied by you, Mr. Grennett—your attitude to me is intolerable—you are hateful to me—hateful—I—I—"

She burst into a flood of tears. Grennett watched her unmoved. Alert as he was for a betrayal, he was not so alert that he heard the door of the office open. Watching her, he did not see the two girls, who stood, interested spectators, in the doorway.

"I hate you—I hate you!" Leah Callington sobbed and stamped her foot in her rage. "You are always saying beastly things and thinking beastly things. You may discharge me if you wish—I came here to work, not to—"

She stopped dead as she saw the girls, then without another word she brushed past them and the door slammed behind her.

Grennett was not distressed. It was not his way. Unconcerned he nodded a brief welcome to the newcomers.

The fiancée of his partner and her sister were frequent visitors to the office, and there was no need for him to stand on ceremony. Nor reason why he should be appalled by the atmosphere of frigidity which the girl left behind her. He was not apparently susceptible to atmosphere.

"Come in and sit down," he said, easily. "I suppose you want Carlew?"

Again he met the eyes of the younger girl, and the pain in them did not perceptibly move him. Yet if any human being in the world had the power to hurt him, it was Doreen.

The girl was the more beautiful of the two. Beautiful in the freshness of her youth, in the glory of her fair skin and delicate features. She had none of the hardness of her sister.

Milicent answered him.

"Perhaps it would be better if we called later?"

"You'll probably miss him. He is a very busy man. One of those men who are too busy for office hours."

The younger girl caught the sting at the end of the sentence and winced.

"Disgraceful!" said Milicent under her breath, but provoked no rejoinder from her sister.

Grennett at his desk was apparently oblivious of any criticism.

"I'm sorry I can't entertain you," he said, as he took up his pen, "my supply of small talk does not thaw out so early in the morning—you'll find some illustrated papers there."

This was a little too much for the elder girl.

"You'll not be greatly surprised, Mr. Grennett," she said stiffly, "that after what we've seen and heard, neither my sister nor I are in any mood for small talk."

Grennett raised his eyebrows.

"Indeed, I should have thought it would have stimulated you in that direction."

"Oh, Mr. Grennett! how could you, how could you! I've always defended you—" It was Doreen, her eyes swimming with angry tears.

"When people said I was a brute?" he interrupted her. "Well, take my advice and don't bother—in this case—"

"Please don't explain," said Milicent coldly.

"I never explain—anything," was the curt response.

The elder girl went on buttoning her gloves.

"As for the unfortunate incident—you may, at least, rely upon us—"

Grennett shrugged his shoulders.

"Tell anybody you like," he said with a smile, "if it amuses you, tell it."

"You may be sure I shall not," she said stiffly. "I should not like people to know that John Carlew's partner—"

Her sister's hand was on her arm.

"Milicent—I don't think we ought to say that. You're really a terrible person, Mr. Grennett. I shall have to change all my views about you."

She sat on the chair by the desk. "You don't realise that Milicent and I have known you for five years, and we are entitled to talk to you for your good... Am I stopping you at your work?"

"No, stay. I like to see you, just as I like to see flowers on Carlew's desk."

He said it simply and the girl laughed in spite of herself.

"You are dining with Jack to-night—and us."

"Jack?—oh, you mean Carlew?"

"Don't you ever call him Jack?" she asked curiously.

He made no reply. The men were co-managing directors, not because they were friends, but because their fathers had left them identical interests in this business.

"It would be ever so much nicer if you were friends—really staunch friends, wouldn't it?" she insisted.

He smiled again.

"No—I don't think so. The only friendships I know worth while in business are friendships cemented by a receipt stamp. Carlew is a nice man," he said reluctantly.

"Oh, I think he's wonderful—so kindly; I don't think anybody knows the good he does."

Grennett made a little face.

"I don't think so either—I don't, certainly."

She shook her head reprovingly, "That sounds rather horrid," she said. "I'm very fond of Jack, and Milicent thinks he's the best man in the world."

"She's probably wrong," said the unenthusiastic Mr. Grennett. Out of the corner of his eye he saw Leah Callington return to the room, and observed with inward amusement the stately Milicent make for her. Moreover he had acute hearing.

"Please don't. It was nothing. Only I'm not feeling quite myself to-day, and Mr. Grennett is sometimes trying... I don't think he means to be, but he is..."

It was on this scene that Jack Carlew entered. He came into the room like a burst of sunshine. From the top of his handsome bead to the polished front of his immaculate shoes he was beautiful to see. There was about him a bounteous happiness which bubbled over: he moved in an atmosphere of cheeriness.

His coming brought a new spirit into the office. The boy who took his coat beamed to the extent of being unrecognizable, for Carlew's smile was infectious. He came over to Milicent with outstretched hands, his white teeth gleaming.

"Hullo Granite," he called over his shoulder—"why, Milicent, you look sweet enough to eat. Doreen, you grow more and more like you sister every day. Now, sit down over there and don't bother me. Watch the machine at work. My letters, Gold."

He saw the typist waiting and then, after a momentary hesitation, he crossed to her.

Grennett watched them. He saw the girl shake her head; noted the unusual seriousness of his partner and smiled a little crookedly.

"And ask them to send me a number," said Carlew loudly. "I should like to choose one without the bother of going to the shop," said Carlew loudly, and Grennett drew certain conclusions.

"Now the letters."

Carlew seated himself at his desk, "Nothing very important."

Gold's voice was almost husky with reverence.

"I beg your pardon, sir," he continued, "but I've taken the liberty to ask you, on behalf of the staff, if you'd take the chair at the staff dinner next Saturday week."

Carlew chuckled.

"With all the pleasure in life, but you ought to have asked Mr. Grennett."

If Gold sniffed nobody noticed the fact. "We thought—well, sir—we thought, to tell you the truth, sir, we thought that Mr. Grennett would be busy."

Carlew shook his head reprovingly. "You ought to have asked, really." He looked over to his partner. "I say, old chap, you'll take the chair at this staff dinner, won't you?"

"No."

Grennett did not raise his eyes from his work.

"Oh, I say—come now, staff dinner," protested the other.

"No," said Grennett, and there was no compromise in his tone.

It was with difficulty that Milicent restrained herself.

"Won't you go, Jack?" she asked. "Of course. What a grumpy devil you are, old man! That will do, Gold. All your people well?"

"Thank you sir, yes. I don't know how to thank you for the kind gift you sent to my wife—"

The lips of the managing clerk trembled. Carlew shook his finger sternly.

"The baby, Gold—don't forget it was for the baby."

"God bless you, sir—I—I don't know how to thank you."

Before he reached the door a sharp voice called him back.

"Gold!"

"Yes, sir."

He turned back to the senior partner.

"This statement of accounts is wrong—did you make it out?"

"Yes, sir."

He bent over, but the hand of the other warded him off.

"Thank you—take it away and correct it."

"I don't know where it went wrong," expostulated the clerk, "I paid particular attention—"

"Don't make a speech—make a new statement."

Gold's face was livid with rage as he went off, and Carlew turned a troubled face to the other.

"I say, old man, you're awfully hard on Gold."

"Hard on him?" repeated Grennett shortly. "He drinks; he's been drinking this morning, or one of my senses is lying."

Doreen walked over to where he sat.

"I think you're very hard," she said gently. "I wish you wouldn't be. When I first met you, I thought you were the kindest man I'd ever met."

He met her eyes.

"Perhaps I am—you never know." Her eyes werc fixed appealingly on him. She remembered how she had told all the girls of her school about him, and how the little dream she had made up around him was all wrong.

"You needn't be frightened," he said, reading her thought. "If you must be frightened, be frightened of dreams; of ideals built on unsolid foundations; of fabrics of illusion—never be frightened of the truth."

He looked up quickly as Carlew came towards him. His face was white and his hand was shaking.

"What is this I hear about your bullying Miss Callington, Grennett?" he asked, and his voice was uncommonly harsh.

Doreen turned to her sister.

"Oh, Milicent, how could you?" she said reproachfully.

Neither the anger in his tone, nor the attitude—half-menacing, half-supplicating—of his partner, distressed the the older man.

"As I don't know what you heard," he said, "I cannot enlighten you."

Carlew brought his fist down with a crash on the desk.

"Understand, once and for all, Grennett, I will not have any girl in out employ brow-beaten and badgered by you. I would sooner end the partnership than allow such a thing. These girls have a damned hard time; it is our job to make the work as light and their hours as pleasant as we can. Forgive me if I speak plainly, but I feel this very strongly."

Grennett's eyes did not leave the face of the angry man.

"Speak away, if it affords you any satisfaction," he said calmly. It was calmness which took the steel out of the other, and his tone grew milder.

"Surely, it gives you no pleasure to make the lives of these people a hell— look at Gold! He shakes when he comes near you. Look at Bristowe—you almost drove him to suicide at the last audit. There isn't a man or woman in our employ that doesn't shake in their shoes every time you send for them. It's not the game, Grennett—it's not the way to conduct a successful business and it hurts me damnably."

He was an injured man. Grennett had offended the world and the offence had come obliquely to him. Thus he impressed one.

"Finished?"

Carlew shrugged his shoulders.

"Yes; I have said all I want to say," he said.

"Ah!" said Grennett, "then I can get on with my work," and he sat at his desk. Carlew waited for a moment, then with another shrug he walked across to where Milicent stood.

"Oh, he's hopeless," he said.

"Is he one of your party, to-night?" she asked, lowering her voice.

He nodded.

"By the way," he said suddenly, "I have put dinner forward by half an hour—you don't mind?"

She did not mind anything he did. She was proud of him for all he had said. It was splendid for these poor girls to have a friend in him, and splendid that he had the courage to stand up to his impossible partner.

Doreen's eyes had been occupied by the momentary appearance of the typist.

"That girl is very pretty," she said.

Carlew looked across carelessly.

"Is she? One never notices these things—in business," he said.

Milicent stood by the door buttoning her gloves. She held out her hand with a smile.

"Till to-night. Good morning, Mr. Grennett."

She favoured him with a distant little nod. Doreen went up to him with a smile.

"Good morning, Mr. Grennett," she said, offering her hand; then, pleadingly, "won't you be more—more—"

"More like Carlew?" he completed the sentence for her.

"I didn't want to say that—but—"

Grennett favoured her with one of his rare smiles.

"Why don't you persuade him—to be more like me?" he asked grimly. "We are all rather proud of our own identities."

"I'm sure you're not as cold-hearted as you pretend to be."

"I'm worse—hullo!"

There was a sound of conflicting voices outside the door, and it was of a sudden flung violently open, and a man stepped in. He was shabbily dressed, thin of face, unshaven. It was a clever face—that much Grennett saw in his quick way.

The man pushed his way into the centre of the room, shaking off the detaining hand of Gold.

"I'm going to see one of 'em whatever you say," he almost shouted. "Now I don't know which is Carlew and which is Grennett, but one or both of you are thieves—d'ye hear that?" He thumped his palm with his fist. "Thieves!"

Carlew was pale; Grennett saw that also.

"Mean, despicable thieves—d'ye hear? Thieves who pick men's brains and pick men's pockets—"

"My dear good fellow." It was Carlew who spoke; Carlew, good-humoured and persuasive, whatever might be the pallor of his face. "There is no need to use this violence in the presence of ladies; we can discuss this matter in a businesslike way."

The man turned with a snarl.

"I'll talk as I like—you've never given me a chance before; you've put me off with letters—you've threatened me with the law—I've had to wait for this chance and I'm not going to lose it!"

He walked swiftly to the door and put his back to it.

"Get away from that door."

Grennett walked slowly towards him.

"Don't come near me! I tell you I'm a desperate man!" cried the intruder. He slipped a revolver from his hip pocket and covered the senior partner.

"I think you're a desperate ass," said Grennett, and reaching out his hand grasped the barrel. He was not flurried, and Doreen held her breath as the man took a tighter grip of his pistol.

"I'll shoot—by God, I'll shoot!" he fumed.

"*Ach!*" the contempt in Grennett's voice made the man wince. "You make me ill with your melodrama!"

He walked back to the desk and laid the revolver on the blotting-pad, then went to the door and opened it for the girls.

"It is going to rain," he said, "I hope you have brought your waterproofs."

He stood holding the door till the women had passed, then he closed it behind him and came back to his desk. All the time the newcomer watched him, fascinated.

"Now," he addressed the man, "what exactly do you mean?"

"What I say," said the other hoarsely, "every word of it. So you're Bully Grennett—well, you've got my gun, but I'm not done with you."

Carlew laid a hand upon the man's arm.

"Look here, let us talk seriously, Mr. Braddon."

Grennett looked tip sharply. "Braddon?—You know him?" Carlew did not answer for a moment, then:

"He's the man who thinks we've stolen his patent," he said with an effort.

"Thinks! Thinks!" stormed the man called Braddon. "Didn't I send you my specifications? Didn't I trust you with every—"

"One moment—is this the pump?" Grennett pointed to a blue-print which hung on the wall.

"Yes, that is the pump."

"What is known as the 'Sweizer Pump'?"

"Yes; identical—"

Grennett nodded.

"Do you know that that pump was sold to my partner and me by a Swiss engineer for £3,000. Now, I want you to discuss this rationally."

Grennett's voice compelled calm, and Braddon lowered his voice to a conventional tone as he answered:

"I know," he said, "that I sent the idea to you in February last year, and like a fool, without having patented it. I know that after keeping me waiting six months the specifications were sent back, and when I went to the Patent Office to register *my* work—I found it had been registered a week after you received it—"

"By Alphonse Sweizer?"

"That was the name—by Alphonse Sweizer. Who is Alphonse Sweizer?" he asked violently. "Has anybody seen him? Have you?"

Grennett looked at him thoughtfully. "No; I was in the Argentine at the time."

Carlew broke in eagerly.

"I saw him, of course. I conducted the negotiations. I tell you, my dear sir, you are altogether wrong; your specification came a long time after Mr. Sweizer offered his patent. I don't remember reading your specification." He looked at his partner.

Without a word, Braddon slipped his hand in his pocket and produced a packet of letters.

"Let me see," said Grennett; then as the other hesitated, he repeated gruffly, "let me see."

The first acknowledgment was not Until March; this much he saw as he rapidly fingered the documents. If this was true, the man's claims were disposed of, for the pump had by then been patented.

"Get me the in-letter book for February last year—letters received."

"It is absurd to search the books, Grennett," said Carlew impatiently. "This is the sort of trouble we are always liable to have. I remember the circumstances."

"I don't care what you remember," roared Braddon. "I want what is right and what is fair. I want the fruits of my brain and my work!"

With a gesture, Grennett silenced him and took the book which Gold had brought back.

He turned the leaves slowly.

"What was the date you sent?"

"The fourth," replied Braddon.

There was another spell of silence broken only by the rustle of leaves. Then:

"Gold—come here."

"Yes, sir."

Grennett pointed to a page.

"There is an entry here—letter from Pike *re* Siberian Exploration Syndicate?"

"Yes, sir."

"A little further down—the same entry. Did you receive two letters in one day?"

"If it is there, sir."

"Did you?"

"If it is there, sir."

"The first entry is written over one which has been erased."

Gold braced himself. "May I look, sir?" he asked faintly.

"Certainly."

For the space of twenty seconds Gold examined the entry, and those who watched saw his weak mouth trembling.

"Oh, yes, sir; that was a mistake. It often happens that one enters a letter wrongly."

Grennett nodded.

"Yes; then one runs a pen through it—like this and this, but you don't take the trouble to erase it."

He walked to his desk, took up a reading glass and inspected the entry again. Then he put the book down, opened the drawer of his desk, and took out a locked ledger.

"By the way, Carlew, where is Sweizer?" he asked suddenly.

"How do I know?" Carlew's tone was loud and aggressive.

"Hasn't he submitted any other patents?"

"No. That makes the third time you have asked me that question in a month."

"Doesn't he ever write?" persisted Grennett.

"No."

Grennett bit the end of his pen and gazed abstractedly through the window.

"We sent him a cheque for £3,000." he said slowly. "I remember signing it and sending it to you to send him. Where was he then?"

"Oh, he was in Stockholm."

"I see."

"The cheque was a bearer cheque," explained Carlew.

Grennett nodded again.

"I remember that," he said drily. "It was cashed in London. I remember that, too. I always remember where money goes."

He turned his attention to Braddon—an anxious spectator.

"Suppose we took up your patent, what would you want?"

"A fair price," said the man vaguely.

"Don't talk rubbish—talk figures."

"I don't know that I want you to have it at all now," said the man sullenly, and Grennett shrugged his shoulders.

"Then take it somewhere else."

"How can I?" he demanded, "when you've stolen the master patent?"

Carlew took a step forward.

"You're a liar and a blackmailer, Braddon," he said hotly. "I can't understand how you can discuss the thing with him, Grennett."

His partner was writing quickly. Carlew saw a little pile of figures grow into being on the white pad before him. Then Grennett took a cheque book from another drawer.

He tore out the slip and rose.

"So far," he said, "we have made a profit of three thousand, seven hundred pounds on the Sweizer Pump—here is a cheque for that amount."

He handed it across to the dazed inventor.

"Good God!" gasped his partner; but the other still spoke to the shaking man with the cheque.

"Come round to-morrow', and I'll fix up the royalty on future business."

"Are you going mad?" gasped Carlew.

"No."

He walked to the door with the inventor.

"Mr. Grennett, I—I—don't know how to thank you," said Braddon huskily; "forgive me if I've—"

"That is all right," said Grennett. "Come at eleven—I'll have my solicitors here."

He closed the door behind the man and came back to face his partner.

"I want an explanation," said Carlew, white as death.

"Wait!" Grennett rang the bell. "We shall all want explanations, I think."

Gold stood in the doorway, waiting. "Gold, go to the cashier from me and ask him for a month's salary."

"Sir!"

"Tell him I've discharged you," said Grennett, and lit a cigarette.

"But, Grennett—"

"For many reasons," said Grennett, as he resumed his place at the desk. "Mainly, for falsifying entries in the letter book. Braddon's letter came—you know it. I discharge you because you are a thief—"

It was at that moment that Leah Callington came into the office.

"Mr. Carlew—" she began, and stopped as she realized the significance of the scene.

"I discharge you," continued Grennett slowly, "because you are not my partner."

Carlew did not speak; his face was a dead white and his lips twitched.

"The idea of the pump," Grennett went on, "was stolen from Braddon's specification. Alphonse Sweizer was put up as a name to which five thousand pounds of the firm's money—my money, mostly—should be paid. There never was an Alphonse Sweizer. He is a myth."

Behind Leah in the doorway, there appeared a little man, meanly featured, but dressed in the height of fashion. He watched the scene, but without comprehension.

"A myth," repeated Grennett, and the word aroused the girl to a realization of her business.

"Mr. Alphonse Sweizer," she announced.

# CHAPTER II

THE dinner-party at Jack Carlew's flat was more than a social function. It was an indignation meeting of a peculiarly serious kind.

Mr. Sweizer himself was something of a hero, though Jack Carlew gave him little opportunity for occupying the centre of the stage. When Potter—of Potter, Fielding & Thompson—arrived, dinner was almost finished. He had just rejected the offer of Carlew's man to accept refreshment when Jack came in.

"It's awfully good of you to come, Potter. Won't you smoke?"

Potter took a cigar from the proffered case.

"Well, you know what the trouble is—I told you on the 'phone."

"Partly—yes," said the lawyer. "I can't quite understand you. He accused you of theft—"

Jack Carlew threw out his hands in pained helplessness.

"Theft—nothing more and nothing less."

The other jerked his head regretfully. "Pretty bad business," he said.

"Bad!" Carlew almost snapped the word. "My dear chap, I'm an equable quality, but some things I will not stand. I've endured Grennett for five years—his rudeness, his temper, and his suspicions—I've come to the end of my patience."

The lawyer nodded. It was a difficult situation. Grennett, Carlew & Co. were a company, but practically the two men held the shares between them.

Briefly Carlew sketched the events of the morning. He stopped now and again to walk out into the hall which communicated with the dining-room in which his guests were, but returned to reiterate the monstrous charge which Grennett had brought

"M'm. He accused you practically of stealing the design of a pump, and selling that design to the company for three thousand pounds?"

"Absolutely—what am I to do?"

"You can sue him, of course. He made the statement before witnesses. And you say that Alphonse Sweizer—"

"Is here—in this flat." Carlew smacked his palm triumphantly "He's dining with us to-night. He turned up—well, he couldn't have turned up at a more appropriate moment than if the whole thing had been a play."

"What did Grennett say?"

Carlew gave a gesture which betrayed his exasperation.

"That's the damnable thing—he said practically nothing. He just took a cigarette from his box, lit it and said: 'I'll leave you to entertain your friend,' and when I demanded an instant apology be said: 'I'm not convinced'—you know his style— with the man before his eyes."

Potter knew his style indeed.

"Do you want this case to go into court?" he asked.

The other paused.

"No, I don't think I do—I have no wish for that kind of advertising." he paused again. "No—I think we might make him clear out."

"Of the business?"

"Yes; he's fairly well off. Hoards every penny—not like me, up to my eyes in debt."

"Are you?" The lawyer looked at him sharply and Carlew realized his error.

"Well—er—that's an exaggeration, of course. In fact, just now I am rather clear of debt. But somehow I can't make money stick, and I've had perfectly rotten luck."

He rose and walked into the hall and stood listening before he returned.

"I thought the business—anything wrong?" asked the lawyer, as he caught the anxious eyes of the other straying to the hall.

"Nothing—nothing," said Carlew hastily, "only Sweizer is rather—you were talking about the business. That's all right as far as it goes—but what is the business? A thousand or so a year. No, I mean outside the business. I had a little speculation in butter—quite a legitimate thing. We thought the drought in Australia would affect the market, and we bought pretty heavily. Oh, well, you can't be interested."

"Yes, I am, very much interested—so you lost money?"

"Yes—a lot." Carlew was short to a point of brusqueness. "Australian supplies, so far from showing any shortage, were abnormal. The market went the very way we did not expect it to go."

"That is a way markets have," said the lawyer drily.

"We're getting off the main subject, which is, what are we to do about Grennett? I am not going on another day as we are going. He has mortally insulted me—and so far he hasn't had the decency to apologize unless"—he rose and pushed an electric bell by the fireplace—"but he wouldn't do that."

A servant answered the summons. "Have any letters come to-night?" he asked.

"Yes, sir, one."

"Then why don't you bring it—you stupid ass! Get it! I don't suppose," he said as the man went out, "for one moment that he'd—"

The man returned with a letter on a salver and Carlew took it up. "By Jove, it *is* from him!"

He opened it and read:

*"Dear Carlew, I may look in later in the evening."*

"Of all the infernal cheek! If he comes I'm not at home."

"Is that all?" asked Potter.

"That is all." He handed the letter over.

The lawyer read it thoughtfully. "He's not the sort of man to be frightened by threats of proceedings," he said.

"I want no actions at law. Understand that, Potter. The best lawyers settle things out of court."

"Yes; but the lawyers who suggest the settling are usually on the losing side." He rose to go. "I'll think it over and give you my views early in the morning."

"Stay a minute, Potter—you're not pressed for time? I think I hear my people coming along. Yes; here is Mr. Sweizer"—a man's loud laugh came from the hall—"he's an amusing devil. I rather wish he wouldn't—"

He stood up to receive his guests. Milicent was there, a little bored; Doreen, more than a little troubled; the stout Mrs. Grantly, most admirable and absent-minded of mothers—and Mr. Sweizer, flushed and talkative. He was speaking as they entered. He had a high voice with a distinctly foreign accent, and he sported in his buttonhole the red ribbon of an order to which he may have been entitled.

"He is amusing, don't you think?" asked Carlew appealingly. He had seen Doreen's little shudder and was anxious to excuse his friend.

"He amuses himself more than he amuses me," she said coldly. "I think some of his stories are horrid."

"He does not know a great deal of English. One ought to feel sorry for a chap like that."

By a superhuman effort he secured a diffusion of attention. Inevitably the conversation flowed back to the scene of the morning.

It was Doreen, a little breathless but immensely earnest, who cornered the solicitor.

"Isn't it perfectly dreadful—I'm sure Mr. Grennett will apologize. There is a lot that is very—very—"

"Lovable?" suggested Milicent with a sneer.

"Don't be horrid, Milicent."

Milicent perked up her snowy shoulders.

"Well, my dear girl, you go on as if you were fond of him. You can't have any sympathy with a man like that, can you, Mr. Potter?"

"Personally," said that tactician, "I haven't any sympathy with anybody."

Carlew seized an opportunity to whisper a word into the ear of the Frenchman.

"My dear Meester Carloo. It is of the exuberance natural—eh? We inventors! Ha, ha!"

"Behave yourself, confound you, and leave the wine alone. You can give me—"

"Ha, I know!" Sweizer shook a waggish finger. "The Homp! *Mais*," he shrugged, "all English people have two things—money and the Homp."

"Talk of anything you like," begged his host. "Keep off drunken people; keep off stories about—about women—keep off—"

It was a trying evening for Carlew, There was need to restrain his exalted guest; some need to entertain Mrs. Grantly, who desired information about shares, and had the vaguest ideas as to his omniscience.

"But, my dear lady," he protested once, "I'm an engineer—not a stockbroker."

The stout Mrs. Grantly shook her head.

"Everybody knows that engineers use oil," she said with assurance. "They positively reek of it. My broker has written to say—I've got his letter somewhere— that South Baku Oilfields are very promising. If they are half as promising as my broker—"

"Who is your broker?"

"A man named Grahame—I try to forget his name is also Aaronson. Though I like Jews—they are so good to their wives. Of course, they have to be—their property is all in their wives' names. These oil shares," she found a letter in a little gold bag which hung at her wrist, "are worrying me. Listen: 'Your directors regret'— they always call themselves 'my directors'—I think it is so nice, it gives you the feeling that you are in the family—I see you are bored."

Carlew was sick with boredom, but he protested.

"No, no, Mrs. Grantly; believe me, I am only worried by—"

"I know—I know exactly how you feel about Mr. Grennett. A man who had the audacity to tell *me* that I was gambling would do anything. I always say that people shouldn't be hasty in their judgments—I think he's a perfect horror, and I only met him once!"

Carlew's ears were, as a matter of fact, for Sweizer.

"It must be awfully nice to invent things, Mr. Sweizer," Milicent was saying.

"Ah, but I am not proper inventor," protested the little man. "With the pomp it was an inspiration. I see water from a well to be hoisted. I note how primitive. I say to myself, would it not be better so and so? I work it out in my head—I consult engineer, practical. He prepared for me plans—which I do not comprehend—and models—which I cannot work. That is all."

"It is very wonderful," said the girl. She caught Carlew's eye and made her way across to him.

"I want you to get these people away to the theatre as soon after nine as possible," he said, dropping his voice.

"Aren't you coming?" she asked in dismay.

"I'll come on later—I promised to meet a man here—it is rather important." He was a little incoherent.

"Won't you bring him too?" she persisted.

"I doubt whether he will come. I'm going out now to telephone to the office to see—whether he has left."

"The Mr. Gold you spoke off?"

"Yes—yes," eagerly. "Mr. Gold."

"Jack!" she detained him as he was moving off. "Are you going to sue Mr. Grennett?"

"I don't think it is worth while."

The lines about Milicent's face were hard.

"I do, and so does mama," she said decidedly. "It isn't quite fair to us that you should have that horrid charge hanging over you."

He smiled. "I know it's rather beastly, but I can depend upon your believing me."

"Oh, yes, of course, dear—I know it is not true," she said in shocked remonstrance.

"Supposing it were true?" he laughed.

"Please don't be silly."

"But suppose it were?" he persisted.

"It would be horrid, wouldn't it?" she said slowly. "Breaking off one's engagement and all that sort of thing."

"But why break off the engagement?" He was interested in her: here was a phase of her character he had not suspected.

"Well—one would have to do it, wouldn't one? One has to be sensible. Of course, it is absurd discussing such a thing—but purely as an abstract problem there would be no other course open for me."

He was intensely interested now.

"I see—wouldn't love come in somewhere?"

Again he saw the hardness in her face: her voice was almost metallic in its matter-of-factness.

"Oh, I love you very much," she said lightly. "But one owes something to one's friends. Why, don't you see that every door would be shut against me. Oh, but it's perfectly ridiculous to suppose such a thing."

"Where is John going?"

It was her mother's voice.

"To telephone."

"Why doesn't he 'phone from here?"

"The telephone is out of order, madam." Carlew's servant supplied the information.

"They are always out of order," wailed the inconsequent lady. "I wonder how much longer this government is going to be in, Mr. Potter?"

It was at a moment when the party had regained its normal poise that Grennett came in. He was in evening dress, and one member of the party at least thought he looked remarkably handsome. As the servant announced his name, an instant silence fell upon the gathering. He felt, as if it were an icy blast, the chilliness of his reception.

"Good evening," he addressed Mrs. Grantly easily. "Is Carlew about?"

"Carlew will be back in a few minutes," she said sombrely. "I don't think he expects you."

"I don't think he does," smiled Grennett. "Though I told him I was coming—ah. Sweizer!"

The little man wriggled uncomfortably.

"Mr. Grennett," he said with dignity. "After you say so many bad things to me, I do not communicate."

"Oh, come." said the other. "I rather want you to communicate."

"Mr. Grennett!" Mrs. Grantly felt it incumbent upon her to speak. "I think I ought to make it clear to you that we all feel, without exception—" she eyed Doreen severely—"without exception, I say, strongly disapprove of your behaviour to John."

He nodded.

"I gathered that the air was one of disapproval. 'Without exception,' I think you said?

"Except me, please." Doreen spoke quickly, but there was an unmistakable firmness in her voice.

"Doreen!"

"I think you are wrong, Mr. Grennett," the girl went on. "I think you will see how wrong you are—but I neither approve nor disapprove of you—"

"That is all I wanted to know," said Grennett, and turned to the agitated Sweizer. "You are an engineer, Mr. Sweizer?"

"Ah, no; I am not an engineer—I am—volatile—ah, what is the word— dilettante—yes? That is the word?"

"And yet," said Grennett slowly, "you invented a highly ingenious pump?"

"Inspiration," said the man rapidly. "I see water from a well to be hoist. I note how primitive. I say to myself—Would it not be better so-and- so? I work it out in my head. I consult engineer, practical, you understand. He prepare for me diagrams, which I do not understand, and models, which I cannot work, but which are very pretty and interesting. That is all. I sell and go away to spend the money. That I understand very well."

"I know—you told me that in the office in almost identical words. You were a fortunate man." He took from his pocket a fountain pen. "You are also clever—"

Alphonse smiled deprecatingly.

"Ah, no!"

"If you did all you say—you are, Mr. Sweizer, I should like you to put your name in my autograph book."

"With pleasure."

The Frenchman took the pen and a flat little book which Grennett had taken from his hip pocket.

"I don't know whether it is quite regular, Mr. Grennett," protested the lawyer, and Grennett favoured him with a friendly nod.

"Ah, Potter, I didn't see you. Are you acting for Mr. Sweizer?"

"No, I am acting for Mr. Carlew. I don't think it is to his interest that Mr. Sweizer should give you his autograph."

Alphonse would have cheerfully given a hundred autographs to stand well with the grim man. Now he paused irresolutely.

"Shall I not?"

"I don't think I should," advised Potter.

"You hear, Mr. Grennett?" appealed the Frenchman. "It is discourteous, of course, but what must I do? You are of the enemy."

"It is ridiculous, Mr. Grennett," Milicent broke in impatiently. "You never collect autographs."

"No," said Grennett quietly. "But suppose I were to say that this dilettante inventor could not write his own name."

"Not write my name, sir?" The little man was aflame with indignation. "You insult! *Voilà!*" He snatched the book from the other's hand, and with a flourish inscribed his name. Grennett looked at the wet signature.

"Or, if he can write his own name," he went on calmly, "as he evidently can, that his signature is not the same signature as that which appears on either his agreement with us or his endorsement of the cheque we paid him."

Potter drew a long breath: he was a lawyer and knew when he was beaten. It was Milicent, fighting her last fight for her lover, who came to the charge. The wild torrent of words she turned upon the man who had Carlew in his grip, did not distress or affect the unmoved man before her. He listened in silence, then:

"Suppose my motives are the best," he asked quietly. "Supposing I am right—

you can't be right all the time. Suppose I am doing all this for you—you and your sister—that I want to make Carlew straight?"

"Suppose," he continued, "I think Carlew is all wrong and I want to get him all right—for your sakes."

"Oh, please don't insist upon your disinterestedness," Milicent sneered.

"Why not?" he insisted. "Who are you to judge *my* motives? What do you know?"

"I think you are very rude," she flamed.

"I know that you are very ignorant," said Grennett. "Ignorant of the world, of men, of life as it is. I want to save you pain—in a sense. In another sense I want to save your sister pain."

"Me—Mr. Grennett?" Doreen looked at him with wide open eyes.

"You—that's the truth—I would let you all work out your own salvations—but I want to save you from pain and humiliation."

"Why—why me?" she stammered, and could have bitten her tongue at the indiscretion.

He did not answer for a moment. Then: "Because I love you," he said gruffly.

The outraged Mrs. Grantly rose.

"I think we had better go," she said with ominous calm.

"Wait!" Grennett held up his hand. He had heard the outer door of the flat close and knew that the supreme moment was at hand. "I want no dark corners—no nooks—no stimulation of senses to tell you that. I am not ashamed of loving you because you're good and sweet and innocent. Doreen, come here."

Obediently she went to his side. "I want you to believe that if I were inclined I *could* send at once for the police and have Carlew and this man arrested. I can't use the threat to influence you. I tell you this, because I want you to know that Carlew has no grievance—save the grievance of a man detected."

It was monstrous of course—how monstrous Potter knew.

"I warn you, Grennett," he began.

"Warn Carlew—you'll serve him best," said the other, shortly.

"Doreen!" It was the severest voice of her mother, but the girl disobeyed.

"I believe you—I believe everything you say," she said.

"Believe that Jack is a thief!" Milicent's voice was harsh and choked.

"I believe everything," said the girl.

"You're mad," stormed her sister. "You've allowed him to make you ridiculous—to make us all ridiculous. And now you—you—" She flung herself into her mother's arms and burst into a passion of weeping.

Throughout the scene, Alphonse Sweizer had been wandering about the room, looking first at one *objet d'art* and then another; flicking at them mechanical-ly with his large and gaudy handkerchief. At every development of the situation he stopped and looked intently, his head on one side like an inquisitive bird. He was in the party, but not of it.

It was when the conversation strayed back to him that he stood alert and at-tentive.

"Mr. Grennett, how can you in the face of proof persist in your charge," de-manded Potter.

"Proof—where is your proof? The firm paid three thousand pounds for an invention—which was the property of another man."

"But—"

"Which was the property of another man. I have been asking questions about Alphonse Sweizer—Carlew has been answering with the irresolution of a man who has something to hide. Carlew goes away for a short holiday on the Con-tinent—for no particular reason, except that I had gone into the question of the Sweizer patent the day before. Two days after his return, Sweizer appears from nowhere. All that we know is that he had apparently been living in the best hotels on the Continent."

To Mrs. Grantly that was sufficient proof, for to her mind there was no better credential of a person's standing than the label of a good hotel.

"And you ask me to accept this as proof that I am a malignant brute," Grennett went on. "You ask me to reject the evidence of my senses. I have watched Sweizer in my office—here: and I have seen him do things which prove beyond doubt to my mind that he is a—"

He swung round quickly.

"*Garçon!*" he called, and Alphonse stepped forward amicably.

"*Oui, Monsieur,*" he said, and his tone was extremely deferential.

"A waiter—"

"*M'sieur,*" said the confused inventor.

"A waiter! What was your hotel?"

Grennett fired his questions rapidly. There was no opportunity for temporiz-ing.

"De l'Europe, *M'sieur*—I—I—"

"Where did you first meet Mr. Carlew?"

"I—I—"

"Answer!"

"Three years ago."

"At Monte Carlo?"

"At St. Moritz."

"You met him again a fortnight ago?"

*"M'sieur!"*

Grennett seized the man by the collar. "Answer me."

*"Oui, M'sieur,* at Biarritz."

"He paid you to come?"

"I—I—"

"Answer me."

*"Oui, trois mille francs."*

"And told you what to say?"

"Do not answer." It was Potter's despairing protest.

"And told you what to say?" Alphonse nodded.

"Yes, *oui,* about a pomp, yes, I know."

"What is your name?"

"Du Bonnet, *M'sieur,* Alphonse du Bonnet."

"And you lied when you said you were Sweizer?"

*"Oui,* three thousand franc is a lot of money—and my fare."

"Stop!" they were so engrossed in the drama they witnessed that they had not heard Carlew's entry. Milicent turned to him imploringly.

"Jack, Jack, what does it mean. Tell me this man is not speaking tho truth."

"Of course he isn't speaking the truth," said Carlew harshly; then to his partner: "What are you doing here?"

"What do you think I am doing here?" Grennett's eyes were narrowed to slits as he asked the question, and the retort which came to the other's lips was silenced.

He turned again to the embarrassed waiter.

"Ah, *M'sieur,"* said that worthy incoherently. "I am so sorry, but this man—what can you do—it is regrettable—but I have won my little reward?"

He appealed ingratiatingly to Carlew. "You will get nothing from me," said the junior partner furiously. "It is a plot to ruin me."

Mrs. Grantly would have spoken but Milicent stopped her.

"Surely you have something to say?" she asked impatiently.

"I don't want people to believe in me out of kindness," he said roughly. "I want to be thought well of—naturally, I can prove my *bona fide.* I think you had better go—everybody; here are the tickets for the theatre—go along and amuse yourselves—I must have time to think—as for you—"

He turned with an imprecation on the shrinking Alphonse.

"Ah, be generous—it is not my fault," cried the little man, frantic with terror. "I cannot help that I do not invent—it is not my *forte,* invention—even stories I cannot invent."

"Go down to my car and wait for me," said Grennett.

One by one the guests were going. Milicent hesitated, then walked to her *fiancé*.

"Oh, Jack, I'm feeling awfully hurt—how could you—how could you?"

"Don't bother me now, Milicent," he said impatiently. "Yes, yes, you've been awfully good and loyal and all that sort of thing, but I'm upset—don't wait, Potter."

Then, seeing Grennett, "I don't think you need wait either."

"I'm going," said the other gently. "Carlew, start fair to-morrow."

"How can I start fair?" Carlew's laugh was bitter. "People who thought I was the best chap in the world—know me! I'm done!"

"Keep somebody's respect."

"Whose—not yours?"

Grennett shook his head thoughtfully.

"No—I don't respect you," he said.

"Don't rub it in," growled Carlew.

"You asked me—no, I think there's somebody else who regards you as little less than the angels."

"Who do you mean? Carlew viewed him suspiciously.

"Search your mind—you haven't got so far in the slough that you can afford to sacrifice another—love."

"I don't know what you're driving at," said the other sullenly.

"Keep that, and there's hope for you." The voice of Doreen in the hall without, called him.

"I'm coming—I'll see you at the office in the morning."

"I suppose you will," said Carlew grimly.

Left alone, he rang for his man. "What is the time?"

"Just half past nine, sir."

"Half past nine!" Carlew started. "Higgs, get your coat on quickly, don't stand waiting—don't stand waiting, damn you."

What shall I send him for, he thought; then as the man reappeared struggling into his coat:

"Go to—go to—look here, here is half a sovereign, go out to a music-hall somewhere—I don't want you back till twelve, you understand?"

"Yes, sir."

"Hurry."

He heard the click of the door, and watched from the window the departing man. Carlew came back to the table, lighted a cigarette, picked up a book and put it down again. Back to the window he went restlessly, then he crossed to his desk, unlocked and opened a drawer, and took out a revolver. He regarded it curiously.

"I suppose it is a way out of the mess," he said, half out loud. "But it's a damned unpleasant one. Twelve infernal jurymen from the pot-houses and tap-rooms of Westminster asking beastly questions about my financial position and charitably agreeing I was mad."

He replaced the revolver in the desk. Suicide wasn't the best way of avoiding publicity—though life held little for him. Except—he wondered, if she would come. He looked at his watch.

What had Grennett meant?

"I'm going to take all that life can give me—what a fool! What a fool! I wonder if she'll come."

There was a timid knock at the outer door and he walked swiftly to open it. Leah Callington stood nervously on the threshold. He led her hesitatingly into the room, and as he closed the door, he took her in his arms.

"My darling!" he breathed.

She thrust him away desperately.

"Don't, please don't, Mr. Carlew. I ought not to have come—only I didn't want to disappoint you. Let us go out somewhere, please."

She raised her pale face to his.

"In a minute," he said fervently. "Let me help you with your coat. I'm hungry to see you; I want you more than I ever thought I could want you——"

"I'm not staying, I can't, I daren't. Oh, please don't make me!"

He laughed, the old Carlew laugh, cheerful and buoyant.

"Don't be silly, Leah," he rallied her—"it doesn't matter what time you get home—you've no relations, have you?" She shook her head.

"No, I've no relations worth talking about. You want some letters done, don't you," and she sat on the chair he pushed towards her.

"To-morrow will do, dearest. I've got you alone for the first time—it couldn't be a better time."

He knelt, by her side and held her hand.

"I mustn't stay."

"Oh, nonsense—fancy dashing all the way up here and then dashing back again without seeing my room—there. You are a beautiful girl, Leah."

She wrung her hands helplessly.

"Oh, it is absurd my coming here—I was a fool—a weak fool!"

"Perhaps you wanted to come," he said eagerly. "Perhaps you wanted to see me—perhaps I am something more to you than a crusty employer—something dearer than—others."

"You are—ah, don't kiss me," she threw back her head, out of his reach.

"Dear, let me kiss you once."

She thrust him to arm's length. "What do you think of me?"

His eyes devoured her.

"I think you are the sweetest woman in the world," he breathed.

"I only came because I trusted you and wanted to—tell you—how much I felt Mr. Grennett's accusation. I know that you are the very soul of honour," she said in the voice of one near to tearfulness.

"Dearest!"

He caught her in a sudden embrace.

"Let me go! Let me go!" she cried, and sprang up. But his strong arms held her.

"I want you, Leah, I love you, by God, I love you!" his voice trembled with passion. "There's no woman in the world to me as you are—nothing half so beautiful."

"No, no, let me go, Jack."

"I love you, don't you love me a little?"

"God knows I do," she moaned, and then his hand touched the switch and they were in darkness.

"I must," he whispered. "The light will show people I am in."

"Let me go—please, please, put the light on, please!"

"Can I?"

Carlew released her and leapt backwards. In the darkness glowed a red spot of light—the voice he knew. There was a "click" and the room was flooded with light. Grennett stood in the doorway.

"Being economical with your light bill, Carlew?" he asked easily. "That is what I call economy in the wrong place."

"How did you get in?" demanded the other hoarsely.

"Through the door—it's the easiest way. Alphonse gave me the key." Grennett walked to the trembling girl and held her arm.

"My car is below," he said. "My man will drive you to your home. Come back to the office when you're feeling fit." He offered his hand to the girl. "I've got a lot of respect for you; remember that!"

He walked with her to the door and closed it softly behind her. Then he came back to the man.

"I'll never forgive you!" hissed Carlew, mad with rage.

Grennett smiled.

"You! Forgive!" His left hand shot out and Carlew went down to the floor with a thud.

# CHAPTER III

THERE was no cheer in the atmosphere of Grennett, Carlew & Co., on the following morning.

Grennett was unchanged; but then Grennett could never change, save for the better. Everybody was agreed as to this—everybody who was in the big outer office.

He made no comment when he learnt that Leah had not put in an appearance.

When later she did arrive, not in the conventional way, but as a visitor, he received her courteously.

There was an especial reason why she should claim his interest

"I'm not coming again," were her first words.

"Why shouldn't you?" he asked.

Then as she would have spoken he stopped her. "Listen, I am responsible for you—not in the way you think. I brought you here. It was I who made you a stenographer—do you know that your father wrote to me some months before his death and asked me to look after you?"

She shook her head wonderingly.

"I didn't know that."

"He used to be associated with this firm," he said gently; "in the days of my father. He always retained an interest in our welfare, and we in his. Now, my child, you see how I am embarrassed. I should be false to your father if I let you out of my sight."

She shook her head, averting her face. "I can't stay—you know I can't stay."

"You can finish your week out anyway. I am not going to allow you to leave hurriedly. To leave at the same time as Carlew may be leaving."

She turned, startled.

He nodded.

"He may—I don't know yet."

She rose.

"Mr. Grennett—you haven't been unkind to Mr. Carlew because of me?"

"Unkind—I'm never unkind to anybody." He smiled a little hardly. "Do you imagine I would do anything so terrible. Now please don't say any more. Have your machine put in the inner office where Gold used to be."

He walked to the door with her. Then he returned thoughtfully to his desk. He looked at his watch. He had an appointment with Braddon at eleven, and punctually to the minute the seedy man was announced.

He looked embarrassed and stood twisting and turning his hat in his hand.

Grennett looked at him curiously.

"Sit down," he said.

The man shook his head.

"Mr. Grennett," he said slowly, and with evident effort. "What do you think of a man who sets himself out to rob his partner?"

Grennett frowned,

"I don't quite follow you."

"I came here the other day and used some pretty bad words to you," the man went on. "I was sore and a sore dog barks pretty promiscuously. I called you thieves."

He paused, his eyes on the carpet, then with a gulp came the truth.

"Mr. Grennett, I am not the inventor of the Sweizer Pump."

There was excuse for Grennett's exasperation.

"Now, what the devil do you mean?" he demanded, rising. "Wait a minute," he rang the bell. "I want this question of the pump and its invention cleared up for good."

Leah came in, note-book in hand.

"I want you to take down what Mr. Braddon says—you don't object?"

"No, no, I want the thing put straight as much as you do. It's been on my mind ever since you spoke to me about my partner." The man was labouring under some stress of emotion. "He's dead. He was a clever chap in a different class to me, but he drank and got into all sorts of trouble."

He told the story jerkily. Mr. Braddon was not an expert in confession.

"I met him when he and I were fitters at the Salt River Works, in Cape Town. When he was sober he was a brilliant man; when he was drunk he was a holy terror. He shared my lodgings; he'd been knocked out of every decent boarding-house from Observatory to Kloof Street; it was in my lodgings that he died. He was sober when he planned this pump: as a matter of fact, I suggested the idea roughly, though I hadn't the genius to properly invent it. I only saw its need, he saw the way to fulfil that need. We worked away in our spare time—I built the models on his specifications. He was a new man in those days—we signed mutual agreements, me to take a third share in the invention. He wanted his two-thirds for his daughter. Why, the very day that he went out on the drinking bout that led to his death, he said to me, "Braddon, this little pump is going to undo a lot of the harm I've done: it's going to bring ease and happiness to my little girl.""

The girl at the desk had stopped writing, her drawn face was turned to the speaker, and the hand which lay on the table trembled.

"Where does she live?" asked Grennett, breaking the silence. Braddon shook his head.

"He never told me—he died that night. But I could have sought her out: you could have told me."

"I?" Grennett was genuinely surprised.

"Yes it was you—Grennett, Carlew & Co., that he told me to send the invention to. That is why I took no precautions."

"What was his name?" asked Grennett quickly.

"Tom Callington."

"Callington!" gasped Grennett. "Good God!"

His eyes wandered to the girl who sat with bowed head.

"Is that—?" whispered Braddon.

Grennett nodded.

"His daughter—? Yes."

* * * * *

"I've made a pretty mess of life, Grennett—I wonder if you'll believe me when I say that, thief as I have been, I do not regret anything so much as I regret my behaviour last night. I wish you had killed me."

It was Carlew. He had come to the office with the intention of removing his private papers. After the exposure there was nothing for him but an ignominious retirement.

"Painful?"

"A little, bit, but the pain isn't there—not the worst pain. I lost something last night—the faith of two good women."

Grennett made no answer and his partner went on.

"Milicent broke off the engagement, of course. I didn't expect she would do anything else. I don't mind that so much—"

"Why are you collecting those things of yours?" asked Grennett suddenly.

"I'm going away. I leave for South Africa on Saturday."

"I know South Africa rather well," said Grennett quietly. "But I do not know that there is anything in its climate which is likely to make you any more useful at the Cape than you are here."

"I'll try anyway," said the other.

"Try here."

Carlew, sorting his letters at the desk, looked up.

"Here—in England?" he asked incredulously.

"In this office—start fair here. You owe the firm three thousand pounds— stay and work it off. Half of it is yours anyway. I am a business man—you're an asset to the firm—why should I allow you to direct your energies in channels which are less profitable to Grennett, Carlew & Co.?"

A faint flush came to Curlew's face.

"You don't mean—"

"I mean what I say—stay on. Forget all that has happened. Put your back into the work. Make money for yourself, and for me. I am frankly selfish."

The man's head dropped to his breast.

"You—you shame me, Grennett," he he said in a low voice. "Your bigness makes me feel mean and beastly. And I can't stay."

"Rot!"

"I can't—" Carlew shook his head. "Though from the bottom of my heart I thank you. There—there is something else. I—I love Leah Callington."

Grennett eyed him keenly.

"You love her? Enough to marry her?"

Carlew nodded.

"You know what you are saying—the daughter of a drunken engineer—a typist—penniless?"

"I know all that."

Grennett thought for a moment, then:

"You will find Miss Callington in the inner office," he said, and smiled as the door closed behind the other.

A telephone message brought Doreen to the office. In a few words he explained the changed position—Leah Callington was a rich woman, but he did not emphasize that point.

"Jack never loved your sister," he said. "There was always another—there always is another somewhere in the background, and I hope and believe that he is going to be happy."

"Do you mean that?"

"Oh, yes, I mean it."

"Are you—are you going to forgive him?"

"On terms, yes," said Grennett cautiously. "I'm a business man."

"You're a business humbug; why, behind that stern face of yours—"

"Is a heart of gold—if I may take liberties with my anatomy."

"And I just hate to hear people talk about you," she said reprovingly. "Your bad temper, your grumpiness, and your sharp tongue. I just long to say, 'I know

Bill Grennett—"

He laughed. In happiness he was a new man.

"Bill is not my name, but let that pass."

"It ought to be Bill," she smiled. "If you behave like Bill—I know Bill Grennett—he's a real good sort."

"I'm glad you don't," said Grennett, as he slipped his arm round her waist and drew her to his breast. "They'd probably come along and borrow money from me."

## THE END

Lector House believes that a society develops through a two-fold approach of continuous learning and adaptation, which is derived from the study of classic literary works spread across the historic timeline of literature records. Therefore, we aim at reviving, repairing and redeveloping all those inaccessible or damaged but historically as well as culturally important literature across subjects so that the future generations may have an opportunity to study and learn from past works to embark upon a journey of creating a better future.

This book is a result of an effort made by Lector House towards making a contribution to the preservation and repair of original ancient works which might hold historical significance to the approach of continuous learning across subjects.

HAPPY READING & LEARNING!

**LECTOR HOUSE LLP**
**E-MAIL:** lectorpublishing@gmail.com